Broken Dragons

AUTHOR BRUCE DALBRACK has lived and worked in Hong Kong for ten years. Originally from Edinburgh, he travelled widely in China and Asia after finishing a PhD in psychology from the University of St Andrews, Scotland.

Broken Dragons

Bruce Dalbrack

BROKEN DRAGONS
© 2004 Bruce Dalbrack
ISBN 962-86740-3-x

Typeset in Adobe Garamond by Alan Sargent
Printed in the United Kingdom and the United States

Inkstone Books (a division of Chameleon Press) http://inkstone.chameleonpress.com
23A, 245–251 Hennessy Road, Hong Kong

preface

Broken Dragons is based on real-life conflicts and events and real people.

Where possible I recorded the words as they came in interviews. However, stories were deliberately mixed with others and also with reports from the media. In short, everything is based in fact but should be considered a fictional kaleidoscope; more was disguised than just names.

My overall goal was to unveil general realities of conflict and corruption. I did not set out to describe specific victories or injustices, or to set the record straight on behalf of others.

My motivation in talking with so many people was two-fold. First, I wanted to give a voice to those who have faced injustice and, in some instances, emerged with solutions and adjustments that are worth listening to. I think we all stand to learn from others that have been hardened by China and how they have changed or been changed. There is something unique and often charming about the way problems of whatever nature are negotiated in China.

My second motivation, however, went a little further and concerned how 'comfortable' people in China, however you wish to define that, respond to the tragedies around them. China is not unique. People in every part of the world face their tragedies, sometimes with considerably less success than in China. But any neutral observer would have to note how dramatic a gap is emerging in China between people who are well-off and healthy versus the mass of people who are poor and ignored, often hungry and having minimal health care and even fewer prospects. For myself, interviewing and talking with Chinese people, I was particularly struck by the detachment that many of the comfortably rich show to what is happening in the daily work and lives of uncomfortably poor individuals and families. In the stories within *Broken Dragons* I hope there are some pointers on how the rich might react if they too were to face problems with corruption and personal tragedy.

I set a very loose time-frame of 'within living memory'. This meant that some events did span as far back as the 1950s and the dreadful clashes of the anti-rightist campaign. The no-less dreadful Cultural Revolution of the 1960s and the anti-Confucius campaign of the 1970s also appeared. In practice, people tended to focus on events since the late 1980s when China re-opened for business. This latest period of China's history has seen the appearance of a new openness, often inauthentic but just as often well-intentioned. Progress towards transparency can only be called a start but for a country so large and so diverse it is already an impressive achievement.

Throughout the landscape I saw, in ways sometimes shocking and ways sometimes humorous and very appealing, a single truth: corruption and conflict are central to modern China pretty much wherever you look.

Depending on your point of view this may be good, or bad, or simply unavoidable. But conflict is, and always has been, a fire that can mould greatness. There is hope that despite China's current ensnarement in corruption it will still create great achievements and all types of great people; great disorder may indeed lead to great order.

preface

This point was wasted on neither Confucius — who questioned if unchanging men ever found happiness and wisdom — nor sociologist Charles Horton Cooley, who observed this more straightforwardly: *When one ceases from conflict, whether because he has won, because he has lost, or because he cares no more for the game, the virtue passes out of him.*

BRUCE DALBRACK
HONG KONG

Acknowledgements

Many people helped in the creation of this book. Those who described traumatic conflicts in their lives, often with little thought for themselves, have my greatest appreciation. I cannot name them, for my word was given to preserve anonymity, but I hope they recognise something of themselves in these pages and take satisfaction that others may benefit from their troubles.

contents

the cities

the countryside

the rich

the poor

the young

the old

From the Emperor down to the masses of the people,
all must consider the cultivation of the person
the root of everything else
Confucius

What you do not want others to do to you,
you shall do to others
Mao Ze-dong

the cities

Flowing into the cities in a seemingly constant tide from the countryside, China's migrant workers already number over a hundred million and many are soon trapped on the wrong side of a supply-demand curve, forced to accept terrible jobs and conditions. Meanwhile, overseas businessmen are also making their homes in Mainland cities, and facing a different set of challenges.

FEI-YIN, female factory worker, 26

Guangzhou, southern China

'I was still working out how to write the words to tell Mama and Papa that Pei-yin had died when the explosion happened.'

THE SUMMER my sister and I travelled to Guangzhou was probably the most hopeful time of our lives.

The economic situation in our home village was not good. Like a lot of the southwest, life was forever becoming more difficult for poor farming people.

But the coastal cities looked quite different, full of life-changing opportunities for both workers and Party members. Though we loved the mountains and the waterfalls, the natural beauty of our county is very wonderful, my sister and I were willing to leave that, at least for a few years. We truly believed we could share in the coast's prosperity.

The train ride to Nanning was very exciting. Our furthest away from home up to that time. The living style of the villages and towns we passed seemed very different to Guizhou Province.

But with little money in our pockets we couldn't keep travelling by train and we had to take a bus from Nanning to Guangzhou. It was very uncomfortable and cramped. The journey went on for days, a week in the end, trailing from town-to-town looking for passengers, even though they had promised to take the most direct route.

It crashed several times along the minor roads, injuring Pei-yin's back and upper chest in the biggest of the accidents.

Without money we had to beg for food while we waited several days for the bus axle to be repaired. Pei-yin suddenly looked frail and vulnerable with her collarbone bandage.

Getting a job in Guangzhou was also much more challenging than the stories said.

Our papers weren't good. This complicated things from the start.

There were also many stronger workers seeking the type of factory jobs we wanted. We became lost in the crowds queuing and sometimes fighting for work.

For fear of worsening her injuries, Pei-yin preferred to avoid those masses.

After a couple of weeks we were desperate, tired and always hungry.

It wasn't a good situation.

So finding Mr Wong, actually it was him to find us, was a considerable relief. We stopped begging, sat down and listened to his story of good foreign employers looking for hard workers like us.

We couldn't believe our luck. We were keen to start as soon as possible. The employment details seemed quite innocent and favourable.

We were required to work in the same factory and live in its dormitory. That was no problem to us. Of course we had no home of our own. Mr Wong repeatedly assured us that both the employers and our co-workers were good people. He also promised good security measures to keep out unscrupulous and jealous people, which had become a problem in the city during recent times. So being safe at night was another bonus.

We used thumb prints from red ink to sign the contracts. Mr Wong said that was better than writing names and provided more rights for the courts to recognise in case of problems.

Pei-yin was overjoyed, proud of the papers in her hand. Mr Wong told her they were 'required by foreign standards and laws' and it seemed like fate was rewarding our patience and suffering with the kind Mr Wong, a bed where Pei-yin could lie comfortably, food, and a good job. We could start helping our family back in Guizhou Province very soon.

The factory entrance was as beautiful as he described. But the compound itself was one huge system of locks and security fences. It soon became clear that they were designed to keep us workers confined within the compound.

Our dormitory on the north side was reserved for workers from outside the province. It was much dirtier than the one for workers from Guangzhou, which seemed very unfair. It had no flushing toilets or consistent running water.

Being locked in every night was upsetting. Neither of us liked that. It felt like being in a prison.

The production line making industrial plastic sheeting and fittings was also much more unpleasant than Mr Wong said. The giant stamping machines were the worst, making massive noises and bad smells that we had never encountered before.

There was nothing we could do but accept the situation, work our best, and have hope for the future.

On the good side they let Pei-yin and I work together, along with the other outside-province workers. Unfortunately this meant handling chemicals and dangerous liquids for the machines. I often became light-headed from the fumes, though I never feinted as Pei-yin did. And I think the third or maybe the fourth time Pei-yin collapsed was when I felt it was only time before one of us was injured badly.

After a few months Pei-yin had more and more troubles. The chemicals were harming her skin. Her hands became especially itchy and red and I think she was asthmatic as well, certainly she was always coughing deeply and found it hard to catch her breath. She stopped work whenever the supervisors weren't looking. That wasn't often but it brought a little rest, usually when they watched TV in the late afternoon. When they were walking around, though, they were unhelpful and uncaring, always pushing and sometimes hitting people to work harder. They refused to allow pots of tea in the work area, which would have helped Pei-yin. She was always thirsty. Being dehydrated so often was another great burden that Mr Wong placed on her health.

With Pei-yin becoming more and more ill, I tried to talk with Mr Wong. I wanted to ask for better rest breaks and to let her drink tea during the working day. But the supervisors prevented me reaching him. I realised that we had never seen him since our first day at work six months before.

The factory was locked day and night, making it impossible to visit the city.

Even a few hours escape to meet Mr Wong in his favourite restaurant across the street, or some other public places where his supervisors weren't protecting him, was impossible.

And other than Mr Wong, the whole place held no real friends for us. The supervisors never mixed with the workers, especially ones from the outside provinces like us.

Being paid in arrears added to our problems.

In fact it was three months before we saw a single yuan to buy medicines for Pei-yin, or soap powder to clean our clothes. We were told that our pay would arrive three or four times a year, not monthly as Mr Wong promised. Also, ten per cent would be used to pay for food, which had never been mentioned before. For a while, honestly speaking, our whole money situation looked like the sky before a typhoon.

Then came the worst moment of my life.

Opening the toilet door I found Pei-yin lying on the stinking floor, as cold and still as ice. Blood was oozing from her nose and mouth into a dark pool . . . it hardly appeared red but almost black and poisonous looking.

I rushed to Mr Wong's office, bursting past supervisors and finally I saw him sitting at his desk. It was the first time I had seen him in nearly six months. I yelled for an ambulance and medical help from inside the factory.

But he was hardly worried, he didn't even seem to remember who I was.

As I shouted and screamed he gestured to one of his staff to take me away: 'Help if you can when the work is finished,' he said quietly, or some other uncaring words, it's too difficult to remember, and as somebody closed the door I saw him inhale his cigarette. It's an awful memory that still upsets me to this day.

Nobody inside the factory showed respect to Pei-yin's body and when the ambulance finally came I was in tears.

An ambulance worker said the dark blood probably meant bad things were in the air. He didn't know exactly but had some expensive tests that his boss wanted me to buy. I couldn't afford them and Mr Wong refused to pay.

Mr Wong admitted freely to the authorities that Pei-yin had died on his premises.

But he blamed her death on her earlier injuries. As the doctors and the police and lots of other people walked around her body, staring at her black blood, he was repeatedly saying things like: 'She hurt her upper bones coming to the city', and 'How can I be blamed for her bad blood?'

Some of the medical people nodded their heads so I'm sure he had established relations with them and they were helping each other make a truth from a thousand lies.

The workers' representative was no help either. He pretended to attack in the east by showing the authorities our work contract, including its promises of decent conditions and regular food and wages, but faked surprise in the west when that turned out to be useless. The so-called contract only listed different types of food and accommodation at the factory. He said he couldn't protect us if neither Pei-yin nor myself read properly and walked away, saying his job was done to its maximum.

After some days it became clear that Mr Wong had successfully shut up the authorities. A senior official in the Work Safety Department told me that it was 'officially concluded' Pei-yin worked for a ghost subcontractor. This had been proven by the false contract, signed with Pei-Yin's thumbprint, which led to a supervising sub-contractor, a Mrs Chow. I had never heard that name. The authorities found Mrs Chow's telephone disconnected, the address was also false, and had given up.

'If your employer is a ghost what chances are there for high compensation?'

Of course his words were just Mr Wong shedding another cicada skin and made me angry, crazy mad angry, everything bad and negative you can imagine.

I cried a lot after Pei-yin's death.

Mr Wong's cruel treatment and distance made me feel worse when I wasn't allowed to take any sick days or even unpaid leave. Not once did he show sympathy or send people with offers of help. He refused to see me again so I never had the chance to explain my side of the situation and open relations with him.

Meanwhile, work became harder and more hours were added to contracts without any more pay. Leave was cut: 'until the emergency finished'. Nobody knew what the emergency was but guessed that meant no holidays until New Year, ten months away.

I was still working out how to write the words to tell Mama and Papa that Pei-yin had died when the explosion happened.

It blasted most of the factory and the south dormitory. The authorities took a week to move the debris. And the bodies. Twenty-three people were killed immediately. Six were said to have died over the following days, though Mr Wong banned newspapers and television from the compound after the blast, making sure we never knew what was going on.

I thought the explosion would weaken Mr Wong.

Many other workers had similar hopes. Neighbouring workers even rioted against his bad safety practices, forcing open the compound doors in the chaos and letting some workers escape. Even though Mr Wong owed them money they were too frightened to stay.

But I had to stay. I needed the money.

Mr Wong, however, was far from frightened. Claiming great irritation at 'disloyal workers', he emerged on television side-by-side with his friend at the Work Safety Department. He passionately listed long-standing problems with the workers, and how they always ignored his orders to follow safety standards and policies.

Such lies boiled people into anger.

Escaped workers gave evidence of an earlier explosion and demanded that the authorities do something against Mr Wong. For the first time I felt he would face hard times from the law and I could get some money for my troubles and for Pei-yin.

Unfortunately, as you can see, that accident scarred my face and also my chest and upper arms. There's also bad skin below my clothes that I won't let people see. My feet and lower legs were also harmed and my fingers and toes are softening, I don't know why, they keep going red, a little bit like Pei-yin's problem.

Soon . . . well, soon I don't think I'll even be able to use chopsticks.

A lawyer saw my situation and demanded compensation through accusations in a provincial newspaper.

His help touched me. Mr Wong is a split personality, the lawyer wrote, one giving bribes and one taking bribes. Connections were paid to paint a massive slogan on the factory walls that said: APPEAL TO A HIGHER LEVEL IS NOT ILLEGAL.

Eventually one of Mr Wong's deputy managers offered to pay RMB3,500 for a proper funeral for Pei-yin, provided it happened in our home province, and RMB6,500 for my injuries from the explosion. However, I must leave straight away and sign a letter saying I was satisfied with these arrangements.

Seeing such little money the lawyer shouted at Mr Wong's deputy manager — *Fuck your teacher for not teaching you right* — but privately told me that it was the best I could get. I had to sign.

The money went quickly, what with the medical fees and the ten per cent for the lawyer and Mama's train ticket. We're still seeking more compensation, though that's difficult because now I work at another factory where the supervisors are just as protective of their boss and just as demanding of the workers. And I think they're going to sack me soon as well; my hands are quite slow on the machines.

When Mama met Mr Wong to collect Pei-yin's body she started crying. Workers were worth nothing to him! People from the poor provinces didn't matter! Anyone desperate for work was his prey!

Mama's words were so accurate, I see that now. He must have searched the marketplaces for innocents like Pei-yin and myself. He killed with negligence and cruel working conditions caused by his greed. He never cared; he was that sort of man.

Who'll employ me now?

I wanted to help my parents and myself.

Instead I burden them. Like when I was young. And when I should be the main source of income. My family has been ruined by his trickery, by the greed of this city. I wish Pei-yin and I never left home.

When I see Mr Wong still controlling that factory, scarcely harmed by his bad deeds, making money and still on friendly terms with Party members and city authorities, I feel angry. I think of revenge. When I remember Pei-yin he's always there in my heart: the crook who killed my sister and went unpunished.

* * *

ZHU, husband, 39

Xiamen, southeast China

'She always said escape is the best scheme and I should have listened. . . .'

AS THEY RAPED my wife I was flying back to Xiamen via Hong Kong, my usual Friday commute from Taipei. That's how they knew Feng would be alone.

After gagging her mouth with towels they wrapped her wrists in strong tape and inflicted the wounds . . . it's still painful to talk about that aspect . . . they were very uncaring about her body.

One thing that's also difficult to accept, still, after all this time, is that my bad attitude towards the estate management office helped bring the disaster. I regret this above everything. If only I had kept a quieter mouth. But the handover of our new apartment had been as bad as heaven can witness.

The decoration was like a pig farm. They hadn't cleaned anything. The bathrooms looked like a building site, rubble and wires were everywhere, neither toilet flushed properly, windows would not open.

And there was a lot of bribery just to get the keys, partly from the city authorities but mostly from estate staff. Attempts at building good relationships only led to tricks and deceit. They were constantly asking for tea money.

When another set of ceiling cracks appeared I finally gave up. Talking to their faces was useless so I complained over their heads to the main office. The staff looked unable to handle even gate-locking, I said, and the general quality of work was poor. I'm sure I used many bad words. They might have been unnecessary words. I should have kept a more harmonious attitude. But it was how I felt after months of troubles. The city, I knew, was out of my control. But the estate should give me face for all the money I had spent.

Inevitably my words reached the small-potato staff.

We both felt an atmosphere. Feng often said the staff were 'deceiving the sky to cross the ocean', hiding their true intentions until they could attack us and have their revenge. Taiwanese people were also not popular in the area which was another dimension they were trying to exploit. Good efforts to speak sweet words and give presents at Lunar New Year were useless; we could not improve their bad feelings.

So when I found Feng in tears, tied up like an animal in our bed, it should not have been surprising that the estate guards were unhelpful. Their first response was cold and uncaring: without proof nobody could act. The younger one even started to suggest that I caused it myself but I soon shut his mouth.

Feng said someone must have let the criminals enter the estate, or maybe told their bad connections how it was possible.

Huge tears were running down her cheeks. She was very badly cut and still bleeding everywhere so it was natural for me, as the husband, to also lose my temper. I threatened to call their head office with more accusations and that quickly changed their mood.

Finally they agreed to call the authorities, though it was several hours before the police arrived.

A senior figure quickly concluded that bad elements had entered through the south gate. I told him that this was the gate about which we had complained; it was rarely locked. Probably they had climbed up through the electrical ducts, he continued, ignoring the problem of bad staff. But nobody could be certain. Because there was no evidence of smashed door locks or broken windows they could not even call it a break-in.

Feng cried loudly: How could they call themselves protectors of the people?

When one of them questioned if Feng had suffered her injuries from other men, which sounded like a staff member was sowing discord through false stories, Feng finally lost all self-control and started smashing furniture and screaming her genes were as pure as theirs. As she cursed violently against eighteen generations of their ancestors I had to send her back to our bedroom for the good of the situation.

The police left, looking angry and far from sympathetic, and I was not surprised that they never found out who the men were. I doubt they even investigated.

Meanwhile I tried my best to comfort Feng's tears and sadness. It was a terrible moment — my wife raped — trickery from the staff — deception from the police, all in one night.

Since then I have always warned against leaving a wife in the Mainland. Even if she's your mistress or something informal the neighbourhood people find out. That makes it easy for bad people to either abuse her or squeeze you for money. As one of those officials said when they found out I was from Taiwan: *Far away water can never get rid of a fire.*

After the attack my relations with Feng were poisoned.

Seeing investigations fail increased her suspicions about the management office. She started to blame me for having poor connections. A good Mainland husband would not have those problems.

She agreed to live in Taipei for a little time. But the warmth in our love had cooled and we separated shortly afterwards, although there hasn't been a formal divorce. Maybe one day we can be together again. . . .

I really regret not listening to Feng at the beginning. She said I should keep quiet about the problems with the apartment. But I had spent that money and I wanted to speak out, as I would at home, and as she predicted that came back to bite my face. I really should have left the management office with some face. Escape is indeed always the best scheme, just as Feng said.

Instead?

I was forced to sell the apartment at a very low price, the estate office saw to that, and to live with the knowledge of a rape I may have caused . . . so sometimes I feel guilty. . . .

*   *   *

HONG-YIN, female accountant, 42

Hong Kong Special Administrative Region, southern China

'He telephoned a mutual friend, claiming I was a bitch, a stupid woman, and lots of other sexist insults.'

IF YOU NEED EVIDENCE that apologies work, then I hope my story shows that.

Late one evening my boss called me to his office. He showed me a letter claiming sexual harassment. Written by a young and junior secretary it accused an older, much more senior, director of various things. Mr Kam worried it might escalate and so it required, as he put it, handling. People were taking sides and he didn't like that when details were unknown.

The accused, an Englishman called Anthony, had just left for a conference in Shanghai.

While he was away Mr Kam wanted me to interview the secretary and other witnesses. From this he would determine police involvement, if any, plus what he called internal actions. 'Elsewhere,' he instructed, 'bosses might take secretaries alone for yum cha, or drive them home, or touch them in this or that way. But our company has no tolerance for this kind of thing. If it turns out not to be a lie.'

So there was a confusion straight away. Turns out not to be a lie? That was very lawyer-like reservation.

The matter was complicated by another aspect: Anthony was well respected. No suspicion or other sexual harassment stories surrounded him and several thought he was quite clever. Yet everything in the secretary's words attacked Anthony. She was unconcerned about his career or that the police might came into the situation.

But as we talked it through, as calmly and carefully as possible, mixed messages emerged. To be honest, actually, the whole business seemed fairly innocent. I had not met her before, working on a different floor can be like working in a different world, but soon had a strong sense of her inexperience.

Our second interview lasted longer.

She needed to talk things through and I was happy to share her feelings if that calmed her. Eventually we came to a shared agreement that there may have been, as we agreed to call it, misinterpretations from both sides. She couldn't give up on blaming Anthony for some things. But she also agreed her behaviour wasn't perfect either.

Other staff had similar opinions so writing my memo was easier than I first thought.

I agreed with Mr Kam's position that such accusations were of concern, naturally, but noted the secretary had acknowledged untaken opportunities to refuse Anthony's advances, if that is what they were. To this could be added Anthony's strong professional background. Police involvement was unnecessary.

Mr Kam was happy and the matter, I hoped, would rest there.

But although Anthony was proven innocent he wouldn't let the matter rest.

It was clear that he had hostility towards both the secretary, which was perhaps understandable, and to myself, which was very unfair and unreasonable. After the secretary requested transfer to another department rumours reached me that Anthony felt I had gone behind his back while he was out of town. Even though I was forced into that and my memo had cleared him he still cast long faces at me whenever we attended the same meetings or saw each other around the office.

By incredibly bad fate I was promoted with three others to work for Anthony. Excuse my language, but life can be a bitch! Mr Kam believed job commitment would protect me. But it still felt like a demotion, especially when Anthony telephoned a male friend to complain that he was forced into taking me, that I was a bitch, a stupid woman, and lots of other sexist insults. He hoped I would not succeed.

Thankfully he called a loyal friend of mine, that time anyway, who warned me immediately. I've always felt grateful for that because a woman doesn't often get that kind of help in the male-dominated corporate world of Hong Kong.

Anthony visited my office on my first day in the new job, I was definitely not invited to his, and said 'Ms Eu: I don't want you to change anything.'

That was it.

He left with the smallest of smiles and you could feel the ice and that he was still very angry.

As the weeks passed he investigated me. He seemed to enjoy asking my staff how I was doing behind my back Any concerns? Productivity? It was nothing unreasonable but he was looking for problems. As my Papa used to say, he was blowing hair away to find a mole.

Matters reached a crisis when I raised a problem about the billing systems in our Malaysian operations. Coldly, Anthony asked why I mentioned this. Did I wish him to shoulder the responsibility? Was that my kind of management?

It was a very deliberate smack on my face.

I replied, smiling as calmly as I could but being very upset inside, that it was nothing to do with shifting responsibility. If problems happen then I would take responsibility. But he just grunted for me to leave, the Malaysian situation unsolved, and we didn't speak for several days.

Afterwards he made impersonal accusations in team meetings about avoiding responsibility, but he never allowed me or others to speak and it was a very bad time for me.

One day he even joked with a subordinate outside my office that I was the fiercest woman in the company. And after he left I closed the door and cried. I don't cry much but it was just too much by then.

The following day I decided there was no real option left. I would have to handle things directly in a private meeting with Anthony. It was that or resign.

I started with a direct apology, butterflies wild in my stomach: 'I need to say sorry for something in the past. . . .'

I thought he was going to fire me. I was sure. If not then, later. That was what he wanted. But I was determined to be clear about apologies . . . and it turned out to be the best idea.

Angry feelings and resentment seemed to lift away and Anthony visibly relaxed.

We talked about the event fairly openly and reached a conclusion that others in the firm had unnecessarily and very unfairly forced the whole sexual harassment issue on both of us. Obviously we were thinking about Mr Kam but his name was never mentioned. Anthony was quite professional in this regard. We even smiled together.

Anthony started to acknowledge my work.

He cooperated more in resolving problems like the Malaysian one. After a few months he gave me more responsibility in Guangdong Province, which he had previously blocked, and I started to travel to other provinces more. Everything seemed to get better. Eventually, this was after a year or so, I was given a team, with Anthony's support, and reported to a new boss.

Why did the problems end so suddenly?

This is something I have often thought about.

There are times you must apologise to men, and that includes foreigners, even if you think you're innocent. Sometimes, also, women have to smell what men want. In my case, neither Mr Kam nor Anthony revealed what they wanted, but they still had expectations in their minds.

*   *   *

FENG-MING, female prostitute, 25
Shanghai Municipality, eastern China

'He secretly intended to manage me as a prostitute.'

WE MET as teenagers.

Kwan was two years older and always felt special and superior, a really high-quality man. When my classmates and I drank beer, thinking it grown-up, he was already going out for karaoke and drinking red wine and Hennessy xo Cognac.

He was also quick to develop good connections with important businessmen and to share money.

I liked that.

One year he sold fireworks at Chinese New Year, made money and bought dinner for me and some other girls. It was the first time a man paid for my food, so ignoring gossip about stolen fireworks was, somehow, quite easy.

Probably he really had stolen those firecrackers, I see that now.

But we were the perfect 'green plums and bamboo horses' in those days, the ideal innocent young lovers.

I left school early, like many others in Zhengzhou, starting as a cleaner at a seafood restaurant. But my looks were too good. They soon transferred me to the front desk, talking east and west with waiting diners and trying to attract others from the street. I liked that. And I looked good in high heels and a *cheong sam*. It awakened me to how a woman's appearance influences men.

Good tips meant that I earned several hundred yuan on some days. That was more than Papa and Mama combined.

Papa pressured me to find a wealthy husband. 'Good fortune doesn't last. Make plans while you can.'

Papa was a rock for our family. My brother had basically disappeared by then, consumed with his family in Wuhan and rarely sending money home. These days I can understand Papa's worries, which were for Mama as much as himself. He was, and still is, a very good and kind man.

At one stage Papa suggested I should marry Kwan. But by then he was in Shanghai and a world away. It seemed that boat had sailed from my life.

Months later, however, Kwan reappeared for dim sum with some businessman and other high-ranking officials.

He was dressed in a very smart suit and tie, used a mobile telephone throughout the meal, flourishing his gold watch and jewellery as he dialled or sent text messages. He looked more impressive than ever, like a crane among chickens, and my old fascination returned.

When we met after my work, it was obvious that Shanghai's money was finding his pocket. He was even more generous than before and I didn't think to question his motives for arranging better work in Shanghai and his other ambitious talk.

'It would need a lot to attract me away from hundreds of yuan daily,' I said, which amused him.

'Over ten times is possible in Shanghai. And in a city a hundred times more exciting. People don't know they lack money until they have been to Shanghai. Who knows? You might marry a rich man. Perhaps find a foreigner from Europe or America and your life will change forever.'

And when I doubted that he simply promised: 'At the very least, working in Shanghai would allow you to buy a house for your family. Maybe a year, perhaps three, just trust me to be the complete and burning light and there will be no problems.'

The restaurant manager was unhappy. He tried to persuade me to stay, saying that I had enough beauty to subvert his kingdom, he wanted me to be his mistress by then, though finally he accepted my determination and gave up, angrily spitting I should leave all Henan Province for what he cared. Stupid man.

When Kwan and I departed for Shanghai I've never been so excited in my life.

Unfortunately Kwan's accommodation in Shanghai was unexpectedly modest. Six people sharing a worn-out boarding house in the far west of the city. Simple bunk beds cluttered around a countryside-style kitchen and sitting area. The toilet was a hole in the wall where you had a shit and washed it away with a bucket of water; the smell. . . .

On the first day Kwan returned in a bad mood, tired, whispering angrily that tomorrow we must look smart and go to work urgently for mutual benefit and better living conditions.

I should have wondered why I didn't need an interview, or why copies of my travelling papers were unnecessary. Or why he would benefit from my work as much as me. But I was still foolish and trusting and I simply nodded.

Arriving the next evening at the Bund, just as Nanjing Lu lit for the evening, was remarkable.

The Peace Hotel was striking. The parks were alive with people, some doing social dancing or playing music or drinking coffee. It was breathtaking, though Kwan was less impressed and more in a rush. We strolled as he explained.

As you can guess Kwan intended to manage me as a prostitute.

He would find clients. While I made them happy like 'deer in love in spring' as he put it in his dramatic way, he would work tirelessly to find more. Perhaps three or more a night might happen. At hundreds of yuan each, maybe a thousand from foreigners, his claims of good money were admittedly possible.

But I still recall the total disbelief sinking into my heart and my rage at his betrayal. Did he think I was that sort of person? How could an old friend force me into this position?

He knew I could not afford to return to Henan. What a bastard! What a shit!

Kwan was unmoved. I had guessed long before, he said, mocking my flirtations with restaurant customers back in Zhengzhou, my sexy appearance, my previous boyfriends, and lots of other innocent things.

As I ran off, tears in my eyes, Kwan shouted that fate never closed a door without providing a way forward.

Having no money that night, or for days afterwards, I was forced to walk home along Jinjiang Lu, miles and miles in the hot tropical evening and in the high heels Kwan had demanded that I wear. Everything about Kwan was suddenly disgusting and suspicious.

Despite my very bad feelings, though, eventually I surrendered.

Kwan enthusiastically found my first, a young businessman travelling from Beijing, who was a relatively decent *cheung dau jai,* a virgin boy. He even apologised beforehand, which I suppose was God's guilt.

At first I only wanted money to return home. It was simply a phase, something I would leave behind me, and for a time I made plans to return to restaurant work and life near my family.

But Kwan sucked me in. It's been years . . . well . . . I had a baby when I was twenty and I'm twenty-five now.

I haven't been home for one single birthday. Mama looks after Hong-hua, provided I send money and bags of clothes and toys home. I still dream of being reunited. I even gave her a foreign name, Helen, for her father, and started to make honest plans to buy that house in Zhengzhou for us to share, one day. If Helen chooses to study in an outside school, or perhaps go to university, I'll try to pay for her tuition and I really mean that, I'm not lying about that.

Meanwhile in Shanghai I learned the rules, the first being that foreigners pay more, the second being that clever girls like me didn't need pimps like Kwan.

I learned English, too.

Especially the sexy words and prices, which is more than many foreigners know. About the only Putonghua I heard from them was *Ke yi pian yi yi dian ma?* — Can you make that cheaper? Kwan never learned much English and, honestly speaking, I never needed his stupid efforts with foreigners.

Becoming good enough for men to treat me as their girlfriend finally killed Kwan's influence. Or so it once seemed.

Living with those men saved rent and meant Kwan never knew where I was.

Though staying with boyfriends for a long time had its problems.

Once, a German accused me of fighting poison with poison, using and discarding men like him as if they were rubbish. I told him everyone does in Shanghai. I certainly didn't feel bad, why should I, and he started crying and going crazy. I knew nothing but cheating and fucking. I packed and left in a hurry.

My problems with Kwan and his vice, though, didn't end so decisively.

If he could find me as I arranged customers he would rush over and claim loudly that I carried diseases, that I was *er maozi,* a pretend but very hairy foreigner, or other cruel things. Sometimes I shouted back that he was like a *jiu tou niao,* a nine-headed bird obsessed with loud arguments and always wanting to fight. But that didn't help.

I would find ways to avoid him for a few weeks but he always found me.

He had a right to a quarter of my earnings, so he claimed. He'd brought me to Shanghai and this amazing world of wealth. So I should pay for that like everything else in good business relations. Attempts at common sense led nowhere and evidence of my money only worsened his obsessions.

Kwan became so bad that I tried Beijing and other small cities along the Yangtze River for a while.

But none of them were as good as Shanghai and when I returned Kwan found me again. Seeing I had tried to leave the city he created new threats, like informing the police of my bad papers or telling my parents about my work.

I compromised.

I didn't want to leave Shanghai, so accepted Kwan as a cost of business in the city. I won't reveal the actual quantity but when I paid Kwan he definitely thought it was enough for his face. He disappeared, for a time, and I got back to saving money for Helen's house.

But as the years passed Kwan worried me.

No matter how much money I gave, eventually he would return for more. Now I'm sure he'll follow me back home and demand a quarter of any house I might buy, or play other tricks with my family. I still haven't told anyone in Zhengzhou about my work in Shanghai. When Papa asks I describe restaurant work, as usual.

I don't think Kwan ever fulfilled his promise from the early days. Never creating anything substantial is hard to bear for face-conscious people like him.

Shanghai showed me that conflict with some low people can become inevitable once they think you owe them. It's worse if you do better than them because it brings jealousy into the issue. Hardships and fights, all the horrible men you fuck, mean nothing to people like Kwan, and they won't let go.

All I want now is to find someone to pay for Helen, perhaps my parents too, for the rest of our lives.

I won't always be beautiful. I won't always have money to pay Kwan, or attract Australians or Germans, or fly everywhere by China Airlines. I'm sure there's one man out there in Shanghai. Someone I won't need to always fight; some man who doesn't know Kwan and, if they met, would ignore him or fight him down . . . or something strong to help Helen and me . . . somewhere . . . someone. . . ?

Sometimes I can't believe I still pay Kwan. It's so many years since he first deceived me and none of the girls I know do the same thing. He's part of my life, good or bad, just like my daughter, just like Shanghai and its ways, I don't think it will ever go away and one day I have feelings that Kwan will tell my parents, which will be a very bad day.

✳   ✳   ✳

JONATHAN, male diving instructor, 27

Hong Kong Special Administrative Region, southern China

'I should have recognised a gweilo in post-handover Hong Kong under pressure to squeeze cash from his assets.'

OUR DEAL looked win-win.

Andrew had the boat, a real but unused asset, and I had the skills to make money from that asset.

Most of the serious scuba divers in Hong Kong had used *Seacrest* at one stage. It had a reputation as, well, more sturdy than graceful. You know the sort of boat. But it could handle ten divers with gear, legally. There was plenty of room below so it might have handled fifteen at times, more on holidays. Despite pushing twelve years it still attracted respectable charter money and in the back of my mind was this idea of renting it for parties around the islands.

I signed a four-year contract.

In return for 'monitoring' *Seacrest*, technically speaking, and fixed monthly rent, Andrew promised 'near-constant' access. I was also free to run parties. Continuous use was a real bonus and I'd give Andrew credit for honouring this. Living aboard with my girlfriend saved accommodation costs in Hong Kong, and a whole lot more beer money. . . .

It turned out the engines were in poor health. Actually they were fucked.

I should have acted during the sea trial. I see that now. But at the time it was easy to ignore a tiny electrical fault.

'Anyway, boats are temperamental bitches,' Andrew promised me, 'Just like the wife.'

But would the bloody bitches work for me?

Would they hell. They spluttered to a smoky and convincing coma about a year into our contract.

Andrew was suddenly unhelpful, refusing to visit or otherwise lend a hand. To keep charters on track I rented a towing motorboat, no cheap undertaking in Hong Kong and despite the danger of towing in the harbour, not to mention the illegality. Thankfully no major accidents happened.

But bad luck never comes in small doses and other problems appeared: a disjoined diving winch, split wires, a gurgling pump, leaking heads. It seemed endless.

Seacrest was soon a joke. Party charters finished completely and most diving customers moved trade elsewhere.

I remember the shock of looking at my bank balance. Money was haemorrhaging daily for the boat so stopping the rent was very satisfying. Shortly after I moved ashore with friends came Andrew's e-mails, frosty phone calls, and the other bullshit of terminated contracts.

'If you don't honour your commitment to provide a fucking working boat,' I remember shouting one night into the phone, 'why should I honour my role as your money-ticket?' I hung up and it felt great.

There was no physical violence, let me say, no dockside fights or bloodshed on the high seas or stuff like that. But there was still this very high tension that nobody would have predicted a year earlier. In fact, that's still the most surprising part of our conflict; how dramatically he changed.

Farewell went this reasonable and often charming person, certainly not your typical money-minded Hongkonger, and instead there was this calculating crook. It was almost as theatrical as the death-throes of the engines.

Part of the problem, I think, was that Andrew, although semi-retired, still had to provide for his second wife and two kids from that later marriage. Not that he was broke, he didn't hide his Mercedes for example, but I should have recognised a *gweilo* in post-handover Hong Kong under pressure to squeeze cash from his assets.

A related complication was Andrew's very dominating second wife.

She relished curt reminders about how much Andrew hired out for as a management consultant and how expensive water-sports were these days. It became so much one day, whilst Andrew and I were trying to compromise on an engine repair schedule and she was there, hovering around and delivering her financial statements, that I reached a boiling point. I shouted that nobody gave a flying fuck if Andrew got paid HK$12,000 a day, or ten times that. Is he Red Adair or something? It was a bit out of order looking back.

Needless to say it put an end to that meeting. And with it, I suspect, ended any plans Andrew might have had for repairing the engines. But whenever Andrew reminded me that he bought stocks at the height of the bubble or how expensive it was when the kids travelled home by British Airways you could feel his wife's influence. She hardened things unnecessarily and I'm sure that stopped either of us trying to be reasonable.

As the encounters continued to shy off useful solutions, I calculated all the money I had wasted on boat maintenance, including hiring the tow. And that was a shocking exercise, believe me, because it amounted to enough to buy the damned boat! Can you bloody believe that?

When I told Andrew that I, not him, that should own *Seacrest* by now even he looked embarrassed; which made me privately think he knew already.

It was the first time I demanded a refund of past rent. To be honest I thought of stealing the boat if he wouldn't pay. Naturally I wouldn't. Of course I wouldn't. But you can fantasise when you've paid for something not in your possession.

I certainly regret our conflict became legal.

Judgements of who's right and who's wrong sound attractive but, overall, threatening letters and the other beak bullshit are rarely productive. Andrew and I should have quietly agreed to a shared misjudgement, shaken on a figure, and he should have told his wife whatever would keep her quiet.

Instead we tied ourselves in knots about who entered the contract 'knowing it was achievable' or 'without the intention to perform'. And soon, in a very depressing way, it reminded me of my divorce.

Thankfully one of Andrew's other business ventures collapsed, a London society magazine where he was a partner, and he became more open about settlement. The lawyers got the hint and compromised that the mistake dated to an inadequate survey of the boat. I was therefore due back some money, though not everything. Basically they managed to blame someone else, the poor marine surveyor, which sounds rather Machiavellian and deceitful, but Andrew reckoned it was quite common in boating communities. Perhaps.

I'm also sure that Hong Kong itself, the city I mean, exacerbated our problems. This city can infuse arrogance into people. Andrew and I would have acted differently if we partnered in the UK. There seems to be fewer rules here. Everyone is encouraged, at least feels encouraged, to cut corners. We would have done a thorough engine survey and I wouldn't have ignored other problems either. It taught me not to think that Hong Kong people are fair and honest just because there's rule of law.

On the plus side, and now things are mostly behind me, in a legal sense anyway, I'm glad I went through this at a relatively young age. The whole hassle of losing fifty thousand US is something dramatically different from what other people did in their twenties. All the inshore diving in the world is no substitute for that challenge.

The weird thing is that it's a year since the lawyers' agreement and I'm still open to renegotiate. To be honest I've dragged my feet on claiming my money, hoping for an adjustment from Andrew and that we can do something constructive instead of just fight, fight, fight. A goal we once talked about was to take *Seacrest* to the Philippines, diving the WWII wrecks. I'm still hopeful that might happen. That would certainly be better than what it's doing now, rusting and rotting away in a Hong Kong typhoon shelter.

What a bloody waste. . . .

the countryside

After fifty years of the People's Republic, since a revolution supposedly enacted to reduce inequity between rich and poor, and implicitly between city and countryside, the incomes of even better-off rural people are barely one-tenth of those in the cities, and often barely one-hundredth.

PING-YEN, daughter, 28

Shanxi Province, north central China

'The mob chased Papa to our house, led by some cadres and other high officials who had forced their way into the situation.'

THE CADRES often insisted on knowing about bad elements in our area. As if they would do something. Let me say, clashes with bad elements can still cost the lives of people. People go to meet their gods often.

Father was killed in our home town in Shanxi. It is not far from here.

It happened long after they promised openness and fairness to workers in the private sector, whether or not they were Party members. But the people in my town thought differently. *They* thought some people could still be killed as they were during the Cultural Revolution. And so did some officials.

Papa was accused as an enemy of the people. Crazy. All he had done was work on foreign-made engineering machines. But because they went wrong and killed Shanxi workers it was his fault. That's what some shouted, anyway, hours after they exploded and collapsed the roof onto the workers.

The mob chased Papa to our house. The worst thing was that some cadres and other high officials led the mob.

I remember Papa's screams and pleas for mother as they bullied him into the street. Mama looked on helplessly, scared of the shouting people, and I was too. Papa had blood over his face and arms.

That we never saw Papa again meant nothing to officials. They continued visiting our area and asking about problems. But whenever we said anything about Papa they said 'some crimes are natural'. *Natural.*

When we said Party members had been in the mob they accused us of lying and warned us to watch our mouths. They were unbothered that we could not find Papa's body and uncaring how much that upset Mama.

None of them cared even one little bit when Mama shouted that my Papa was a worker like everyone else . . . just trying to make a living for his family . . . simply obeying the owner's orders.

To this day those crooked authorities have done nothing to the owner of the factory, the one who told Papa what to do. . . .

Within a year the mob killed my mother.

'Mourning criminal death too long!' some chanted, though they didn't have the courage to say it to our faces. As if living off Papa's small savings showed anti-people values.

'His money should go to the people that his crimes harmed,' a stranger in the street said, looking at me like I was a dog.

Since then I have seen none of Papa's money . . . the bank account was just closed one day.

I still don't understand why the officials or the courts don't care about the mobs . . . I don't understand how people managed to steal our money . . . how some Party members joined the mob. . . .

That's all I have to say.

*   *   *

GUO-BANG, male workers' representative, 42

Fujian Province, southeast China

'Her cronies threatened the other employees. Workers refusing to commit their pensions were asked to leave the factory.'

POOLED CAPITAL PASSION consumed our province about ten years ago.

Part of *gufenzhi,* changing state-owned enterprises into private enterprises, the idea was to improve workers' lives. But I don't think even Deng Xiao-ping intended it would result in lost workers' pensions; *gufenzhi* for our factory, in fact, was disastrous, nothing but an illegal waste of pensions. And all by a Party member too.

That character was our factory boss, Mrs Yao. She had fallen in love with what other shady characters were doing. Party members like her often act like that, without a single thought for workers they represent and are meant to care for.

Enforcing participation by linking the scheme with New Year bonuses was her first trick. Many of the workers depended on that.

For others she placed bogus blossoms on the tree, promising guaranteed returns of 25 per cent. If you put in RMB1,000 she assured RMB250 a year return. Close to a month's salary for some workers.

Her cronies threatened doubters at large meetings: 'If small sums are not spent, big sums will not come. Workers who still won't commit their pensions might be asked to leave.'

I said it was illegal. For the good that did.

People knew Mrs Yao had used her bricks to trick jade from them, but were too frightened for their livelihood. They had no choice.

The larger the pooled capital became the more confident Mrs Yao became. The saddest thing was people outside the factory, often with no savings, borrowed money to join. They heard all the gossip and ran off to sell their buffalo or other vital possessions. As more strangers became interested Mrs Yao increased minimum investment to RMB4,000 per investor, offering RMB1,000 in annual interest.

She kept quiet from the workers that this would *also* be their Chinese New Year bonus; that extra deception only emerged later.

The money certainly wasn't invested in new production equipment or solving the pollution problems with dichloromethane, which she once mentioned. Those barrels remain today, leaking into the fields and then the river. I don't think that Mrs Yao *ever* intended to do anything about the harm they caused the children downstream. Too far from view.

Instead the money was spent, wasted more like, on building her restaurants and hotels.

Like many top officials she wanted to get involved in sectors with opportunities for bribes and kickbacks; her hope was to pilfer sales commissions or illegal taxes in ways difficult to monitor.

After they finished building shops and the hotel, with little concern if they were actually *profitable,* Mrs Yao went back to some investors. Would they also be interested in some *love business* in the city-centre? By which she meant getting into prostitution, though she didn't have the courage for such honesty. She was just using the chance to steal a goat whilst she was walking her sheep home.

I spoke loudly against that scheme. Others too; older workers were especially unhappy. Beijing didn't allow such businesses so how could she create one in Fujian Province?

But Mrs Yao proceeded regardless. A crony acquired young women from poor families around the Dongbei area and they were in business within a few months.

I suppose it's fair to say that that kind of sex-broking was widespread in our area. But as a Party member she should not have gone against state laws protecting women. Worker's money should *never* be used for decadent purposes.

Notwithstanding her immorality, if the restaurants and the shops and the hotel and the prostitution had worked nobody would have minded much. As Deng said, the colour of the cat doesn't matter as long as it catches mice.

But the problem was that money did not come in.

The first problem was that senior officials 'favoured' Mrs Yao with more of their business than she wanted. Of course she dared not to charge them, despite their offers to pay. If that happened and she inadvertently made somebody senior lose face, inspectors would have arrived the next day, found fault and closed everything. Some days half of her customers were officials and by some estimates two-thirds of her money disappeared this way on bad days. I don't know if it was that much but it was certainly a serious problem.

The prostitutes suffered from diseases and hospital doctors started causing problems via connections in the city health authorities.

Within a couple of years, in fact, Mrs Yao's babies had either failed or were failing. Poor local people even used the ex-restaurant block for sleeping, which tells you how quiet they were.

Nobody received any of their 'guaranteed money' in the first year. For the first dividend we had to be content with payments in goods and materials.

Mrs Yao came up with a creative chart converting money owed into rice or clothing or vegetables. Of course she also tried to quietly collect a sales commission from the participating shops. Workers saying they expected *cash* dividends were challenged to find written proof. Nobody could.

Even the interest-in-kind payments stopped the following year. Mrs Yao never said much anymore and people gossiped that she wanted everyone to forget the whole business, as if the workers would or could. How can workers ignore losing their pension?

When Mrs Yao quietly tried to turn the lost money into what she called *image shares* workers shouted loudly. It soon surfaced that these were both worthless and illegal and would not be recognised by the provincial authorities.

Mrs Yao told people she was upset at the complaints against her even though she had tried her best. The original investment would be returned, if people desired, it was just that it would take a few more years due to the cross-straits tension. She then appeared with a Xinhua report describing how the Taiwan situation was having a negative impact on the provincial economy. Afterwards the workers started to call Mrs Yao the 'human chameleon'.

The following Chinese New Year, when tensions rose because people wanted money for family commitments, the chameleon tried to keep people quiet by giving receipts for their investment. *A share receipt!* It didn't even have 'share' written on it. All it said was that such-and-such an amount had been received without even mentioning for what.

By then workers felt frightened and started to make noises with other authorities.

Eventually this forced Mrs Yao to issue a charter and attend a 'Shareholder Representatives meeting'. Senior officials were persuaded to attend and it looked like she might finally have to face justice.

Officials who had been supportive in the early days were also becoming angry. Several were even speaking publicly about their disappointments, a very rare thing between Party members; talk about expelling her from the Party was even heard. The boss of the Inspection Committee that Mrs Yao had set up was notably unhappy.

Pressure and anger against Mrs Yao was boiling like a wok, hot from all sides.

But ultimately it proved useless because Mrs Yao had carefully built relations with even higher authorities.

'Wait a little longer,' those higher-ups said when they got involved. 'It is not under our influence — which was a lie — but don't worry. Your leaders will sort this out. Like Chairman Mao, Mrs Yao's achievements are primary and her mistakes secondary. The workers must keep good faith.'

But the workers were far from convinced.

They badgered the new faces privately for help. But they had been well prepared and stayed loyal to Mrs Yao. 'Please talk to my department later,' they said, one more trick to delay the situation. Even when we went to see them as a big group they continued to lie.

After some time the workers recognised me as leader of a special committee to press our claims.

I made a written complaint to the provincial Party leader, stressing Mrs Yao made the bad investments without consultation. We wanted our money to be repaid as was our right under the People's Law. The restaurants and hotels must be sold as well and the prostitution place should be closed.

In response came absolutely nothing. It was as if I had not spoken. His office didn't even acknowledge receiving my letter.

Shortly afterwards, though, Mrs Yao announced that because of divisive people's complaints there would now be two types of share-holders. Anyone who had contributed RMB10,000 or more would become a major shareholder. They would be repaid as an urgent priority.

This meant important Party officials because only they had such cash.

For ordinary shareholders she would do her best to pay them soon. But she could not be blamed for bigger economic problems and the challenges being made by foreign enterprises.

Of course this was designed to split her investors, officials versus workers, whilst showing the provincial boss that something was happening to make it go away.

Because nobody could find a higher connection to challenge Mrs Yao we tried making stories against her in the newspapers. One of Mrs Yao's top managers was attacked over a sex scandal at the prostitution place and we thought that would start some punishments. But instead of being sacked or prosecuted, Mrs Yao just relocated her crony to another factory where she had connections.

In revenge Mrs Yao stopped issuing bonuses. Only her cronies and family members received anything the following Chinese New Year. The rest were only paid basic wages, often less than RMB500 a month.

'Of course,' her people would say, 'it's common for workers to be denied payments at New Year these days.'

Two elderly workers who had lost their life savings protested by standing on a ninth-floor building ledge. But in the end they had to come down for food, with nothing to show for their efforts.

Mrs Yao went straight to her media contacts full of fancy stories about the two-thirds of people living in 'economically disenfranchised rural areas'. Those mad workers should be grateful for what they have. Green and yellow often appeared in close succession, she said, trying to make it look like people were just starving between harvests and it would be all right in the end. After the noise died she used the *hukou* registration card system to sack the two workers plus a few others she disliked. Like a common looter taking advantage of a burning house.

And, to this day, nobody has seen much of their money come back.

I still have so many questions: How could the authorities allow one person to harm so many people? And in the workers' name too? Why did nobody in authority seem bothered that the workers lost their pensions? Are we a socialist country? I really wonder. What difference is there between Mrs Yao and the Qing mandarins, whose corruption led to the foreigners exploiting people like pigs? Surely this can't be what modern life is about? Can it?

*　　*　　*

SU-XIANG, female teacher, 31

Yunnan Province, southwest China

'He was using Confucianism to further his greed and to make the children produce more fireworks for sale.'

FROM THE BEGINNING I always felt the other teachers disliked me.

The problem was that I graduated from a normal university. It was quite a small school, only a few hundred children from primary age to teenagers, so few of the teachers had been to anything more than small provincial colleges, never mind a university. Even my two fellow science teachers had no real qualifications. That caused tensions because they were senior by rank and they hated if I questioned their science talk.

Coming from the east was another problem. The headmaster especially disliked my attempts to share Shanghai culture and its 'so-called advanced ways'.

I'm sure he would have sent me to another school if the county authorities hadn't insisted on taking Shanghai people like me.

It soon became clear why he was so reserved.

For Mr Ng, the school was a way to make himself wealthy through the children's labour, which he manipulated through appeals to traditional ethics and Confucianism.

At morning assembly he would say things like: 'We require values shared by the majority. Joint efforts are needed to benefit our school!' The children looked on in a kind of tired awe. It's still hard to describe whether they feared or loved him more, perhaps it was both equally, but it was definitely a very strange and tired look. Children in Shanghai don't look like that.

His favourite practice was quoting classic literature, especially *Romance of the Three Kingdoms.* He would open a frayed paperback and jump on poetic passages that glorified loyalty and comradeship and the integrity of inner circles versus outsiders. In the next breath he switched to reviewing productivity, linking any shortcomings to the importance of harmonious relations and effective improvements.

There were many other convenient lessons he squeezed from those classics. When output of the fireworks they made fell greatly he lectured about Confucian concepts of filial piety, somehow linking this to the *Three Character Classics*: 'Fraternal duty, loyalty and truthfulness', was his pet phrase. 'These create better production!'

The children continued working half of their day despite my complaints. They were constantly in dangerous conditions that I'm sure wouldn't be allowed near Shanghai.

As my talk was having no effect I confronted Mr Ng in writing.

It is both dangerous for the children and against national laws, I wrote: *All children in the People's Republic have the right to safe conditions of study. They are getting less than half of the day to study so how can they improve their minds? Confucius could never see that as a good thing,* I added, hoping to use his weapons against him.

But national laws were not very important to Mr Ng.

Outsiders like you don't understand the whole situation, he wrote back. *You should concentrate on building more harmonious relations with the local people and their children and listening to their concerns.*

When the blast finally came it was huge.

Happening a week before National Day, for which many of the fireworks were intended, meant that most of the children were packing. Probably forty children were killed outright. Many more suffered terrible burns. Younger pupils who did the wrapping were burnt the worst because they were near the unpacked fireworks. The smell of burning skin was very clear . . . children still alive were crying for mercy, pleading to Mr Ng for an end to their pain.

Three adults were also crushed to death when the two-storey building collapsed, though I only counted two teachers as missing. One of the bodies was probably a businessman or some cadre in business with Mr Ng, unlucky enough to be in the wrong place at the wrong time.

During the enquiries I told police about Mr Ng's use of Confucius to force the children into harder work. I added my suspicions that he must be collaborating with a private firecracker factory, though I didn't know any details. The other teachers never talked to me much. When I told them that some other city authorities were probably involved too, judging by their frequent visits to the school, there was a real hush.

Thankfully others outside the school also criticised Mr Ng.

Within a short while, in fact, the police became worried that some parents who had lost children would kill Mr Ng given half a chance. He was taken into *protective prison,* as the police called it, though I had the feeling they were also protecting someone who protected *them* at other times.

When a senior official made a public joke that the accident would help the area meet family planning targets, paramilitary officers were drafted in to control the riots. I was sure that Mr Ng would be imprisoned for a very long time; the mob were gathering like crows over fresh blood.

Mr Ng, however, knew more than Confucius.

First came a public letter. Written with the 'permission of the school authorities and local police,' it said, so he obviously had *them* on his side. Poor parents had always needed children to earn money for school fees. They didn't think making fireworks was so dangerous *back then,* he wrote.

Copies in the local newspaper boards and on the school gates seemed to quieten people's anger and the local police discreetly escorted Mr Ng to a public meeting that he had requested.

Mr Ng was truly enraged at being blamed. He shouted that other teachers were also receiving commission on the labour of the children and read out the amounts paid, followed by the amount of firecrackers made by their classes. A lot of teachers were suddenly quiet. . . .

'Did the parents think that he was the *dushiqiang* element here?' he asked, referring to a strong rat poison sometimes used to kill people. 'Several other local schools also collaborated with local firework factories!'

Mr Ng returned to school the next day, seemingly unaffected by the deaths of the children.

A few months on I was asked to leave. To make way for different courses, was Mr Ng's official explanation, but that was a lie to keep the county authorities happy.

I knew he would put the children back to work, but what could I do? Parents seemed content with promises of fire extinguishers in each classroom, for what good that could do . . . others were seemingly content with Mr Ng's statement that sometimes the plum tree must be sacrificed for the peach tree.

I remember Mr Ng once said: 'People have a desire to depend on something, to be drawn to something strong. This is Confucianism in action. Accidents are tests that create character.'

And I'm sure some of the parents eating with us that day, even those who'd lost children, nodded in agreement. Terrible!

Mr Ng taught me that people can easily abuse Confucius to make profit or advantages for themselves, pretending things are for the common benefit. And very often these people have good relations with the authorities. 'Do your utmost so that social cohesion is maintained,' he used to tell the children. What a lie . . . what a tragic lie.

*   *   *

KA-PING, male mechanical engineer, 36

Jiangxi Province, eastern China

'He was cheating people's good faith. The false stories concerning his abilities and qualifications were like a new soul in a dead body.'

ZHENG AND I went to school together and then to Technical University, so we were classmates for at least 15 years.

He wasn't as clever as some, or tidy in appearance, because his family were quite poor.

But we had good relations. Being a little brighter I helped him if I could, especially showing him what to remember for examinations and taking him to auto-repair garages to better understand engines. Small efforts, perhaps, but you should look after the less fortunate if you can.

Zheng, however, excelled in speaking English.

Even before we left school he could have conversations with foreign tourists at Bai Hua Zhou, the Hundred Flowers Island. Soon he was speaking well enough for the foreigners to buy him beer and noodles and change money. Later he started taking foreigners to souvenir and craft shops, which meant tea money from the owners. I wouldn't call it wrong, it wasn't against the law, but it showed Zheng also had a cunning side.

Our connection continued into our twenties. We attended each other's weddings and had our children at similar times. Generally were very aware of each other and our families. We talked on friendly terms often.

Unfortunately, though, we lost touch when Zheng took his family to Fuzhou.

His parents told me later that he found good work with an American or maybe a Taiwanese company, they did not know for sure. I assumed we would not see each other again for a long time.

Meanwhile I continued working in Nanchang, becoming an honest and important deputy engineer with good prospects. Jiangxi is a good province for hardworking and truthful people like me. My mechanical engineering qualifications and awards earned great respect, especially during the early eighties and the era of the Sixth Five Year Plan.

I sometimes thought about Zheng, wondering what had happened to him and his family. But I never predicted my fate. Zheng's company, it was American after all, bought an important stake in our factory and appointed Zheng head manager. He was responsible for eighty staff, including myself, many of whom he had last known ten years before as friends and equals.

Zheng acknowledged me very briefly on his return.

He was seemingly neutral about renewing our relations. Instead he was more enthusiastic in seeking others around the factory and in the local authorities that were better connections.

I sent a small bottle of cognac to celebrate our past friendship and ensure good communication channels still existed. However I received nothing dignified back. Only his secretary acknowledged the gift verbally and that was not a good sign.

He was more showy than the old days. Often he wore Japanese or American-style clothes and baseball caps, showing off money and gold jewellery whenever he could.

A few months after he came back he ordered the factory to buy a luxury Volkswagen car. 'For general management use,' he informed people. Yet the driver usually served Zheng and his family: his daughter was chauffeured daily to school; his mother used it for hospital visits; and it was his connections and friends that used it for karaoke parties or day trips to Poyang Lake.

I acknowledge the boss deserves privileges. But Zheng denied other managers their rightful use of the car, treating himself like a special Party official or some other higher-up, rather than one of us that had been lucky. It felt like a very bad example for the local people.

Zheng was also telling lies about himself.

The worst false story concerned his engineering qualifications, which were like a new soul in a dead body.

When some visiting investors from Fuzhou publicly proclaimed their support for Zheng and his *excellent knowledge and award-winning academic background,* I sought a meeting to clarify the situation. It seemed very unfair to others who had done well in their studies and I hoped he would give me better recognition.

Zheng pretended not to remember much.

'Many things have changed,' he finally said, dramatically, 'I am now a businessman dedicated to making our country profitable. Old ways and thinking have to change.'

When I mentioned our past, and how that had made great things possible for him, he became cold and vague, saying he needed to go. His claimed awards and qualifications were never mentioned but I'm certain he got my point.

That must have been when he decided to act against me. After a few weeks some of his managers came to look at my section's responsibilities, which were soon reduced. 'Necessary for survival,' the manager claimed, but I felt it was Zheng showing who had the bigger knife and the broader axe.

I shared my confusion with the manager, knowing that some of my words would reach Zheng. My team had performed well for many years. It had delivered good service to the people of the province and to the company. Furthermore, I added, many *others* were weaker in their qualifications yet strangely none of them had been cut or harmed. I was confused why they still had face. Why were we attacked?

Eventually I went to Zheng and it was the last time we met privately.

I suggested a good person should respect past associations. I knew his real strengths and history but had said nothing to anyone, allowing him to keep good face. Yet he allowed his managers to treat me like the son of a rabbit and ignored my requests for meetings.

Zheng smiled but was unmoved.

After a few sweet-mouthed words about investigating further he said that I must leave as he was busy.

I had my feelings what that *really* meant.

In the coming weeks managers started to say things like: 'You people don't understand pressure', 'Everyone must modernise for future success' and 'If you can't accept new thinking then you should run away'.

Zheng's biography quietly changed. Company brochures were revised and people were informed he attended 'various education institutions at different times' to accumulate his knowledge, not just places in our city.

Meanwhile quality at the factory suffered and the American side became unhappy at their investment. But people said they couldn't sell due to some legal problems caused by weak relations in the area. Frustrated, they forced the plant to cut one-in-ten of the staff. My section was finally dismissed altogether.

It was one of the toughest times in my life.

I had been promised the job for my life and it *was* my working life until then. But eventually I felt better. To tell the truth I had suffered more and more unhappiness at the factory. Whenever I saw Zheng in his expensive car or surrounded by officials as he toured the production line, it made me want to shout angry words and did my health a great disservice.

I felt better telling people about his deception but my regret is that I can't do much against him. I still have to work at a new job and it is easy to look like a complaining and jealous child, you must be careful these days because *guanxi* is so strong and there is no telling what they might do.

But I still hope that someone might find a safe way to fully reveal Zheng's wrongdoings.

They might write anonymously to his superiors in Fuzhou, about how he called a pig a stag, or they might make life difficult for his family amongst their neighbours, or other things.

People should avoid my mistake of thinking private meetings and informal words solve problems. Sometimes they just help powerful people make more lies and strike back hard. Don't think that lying people automatically pay the price, either, because Zheng is one more proof that the bigger liar often creates the bigger opportunity . . . large pigs and long snakes often get their way.

*　　*　　*

KEUNG, male printer, 32

Fujian Province, southeast China

'We would have to submit to unknown punishments unless we paid him RMB50,000 to make the problem disappear.'

WE WORKED for that cheating official for a long time.

We did brilliant work. He ordered more and more fake certificates that he sold through his backdoor methods. We were promised that he would keep the authorities quiet.

Our boss was always careful to charge small sums, paid in cash, and to give a little money back for the cadre's face. Even though the documentation was so good experts couldn't tell the real from the fakes, sometimes.

But despite his promises never to record our name, when the police arrested that cadre they found mentions of our factory in his paper-work. Addresses were in his diary. So they knew where the fakes had been printed and the police and anti-counterfeit authorities quickly came to investigate.

Very aggressively, they demanded to know why we had associated with such bad elements.

My boss was really pushed hard and they started to hit him in the head as everyone watched. It looked like real violence would happen.

A senior official accused everyone in the factory of shared guilt in cheating the people and other serious offences. No exceptions or excuses, he shouted angrily. He threatened a lot of bad things could happen to us and we must stop illegal printing immediately. The boss must also write a self-criticism about the errors of working for corrupt elements, though he was careful not to say 'corrupt officials'.

As unexpectedly as they arrived, though, the senior official and the others received a phone call and disappeared with his juniors, not even waiting for the self-criticism letter and leaving us to question what had just happened. It was as if we had only had a bad dream.

Shortly after another cadre arrived with an answer to our confusion.

He said he was from the same department as our corrupt official, though he wouldn't show any documents or identity papers. He claimed to have persuaded the police to leave due to his connections. But they might be back, he threatened everybody, menacingly, like a tiger stalking a chicken.

And he was certain if that happened, one prick of his needle would draw all our blood and we would have to visit the police station and submit to unknown punishments. Unless, that is, we paid him RMB50,000 to make the problem disappear completely.

My boss argued we were only doing work that his colleague had commissioned, anyway. Just poor workers making a living. 'So how can we be punished for the original fraud within the Party?' he asked.

Our tiger was unmoved.

After negotiation apparently RMB30,000 was paid as a bribe, which our boss said would mean less money in everyone's bonus. Some of us had suspicions whether the bribe really was so much money. But we were left with no choice and accepted events to keep our jobs.

the rich

China's economy has grown annually at around 7.5 per cent for the last decade, creating an increasing number of rich people. Many have become so targeted by scalpers that they complain openly of 'economic warlords' in the Party; officials have embezzled millions, sometimes billions, of yuan from wealthy people or joint ventures. Mao's slogan: 'Serve the people' may once have ruled their hearts. But faced with so many temptations their hearts have clearly heeded a more traditional adage: 'Make the best use of power whilst still in office'.

CHARLES, male investment banker, 33
Hebei Province, northeast China

'Losing US$7 million with nothing to show for it except a lot of headaches is a very expensive lesson.'

SINCE THE EIGHTIES I guess two-thirds of manufacturing joint ventures like us have lost most, if not all, their investment. Many have discovered, just like we did, that local partners can slip into the shadows and prove very difficult to find when trouble happens.

Our joint venture joined an American computer parts manufacturer, quite large and traded on the New York stock exchange, with a state-owned assembly factory. Casings and plastic fittings for laptop computers aren't especially hi-tech or sexy, but the works employed several hundred technicians and provided useful opportunities for local distributors. The Americans liked it enough to purchase 49 per cent for several million dollars, repayable within ten years.

My involvement was to arrange finance for the 51 per cent local ownership.

Eventually this was shared between a commercial arm of provincial government (12.5 per cent); a Shanghai-based consortium that claimed to have very senior connections in Beijing (13.5 per cent); and Mr Lu, a fairly prominent matchmaker of state assets with foreign investors (25 per cent).

The 51 per cent was wrapped within a British Virgin Island trust. To this was made the initial — and final — loan of US$12 million. This contracted for three years of operations at around US$250,000 per month. Repayment was to be within ten years, and the profit . . . well, that proved meaningless.

The CEO proved hopeless, a Mr Zhou from the provincial authorities. Deadlines were meaningless, he worked when and to what schedule he wanted. Staff training and development was non-existent and quality went on an apparently unstoppable slide.

Within a few quarters production barely covered loan repayments, let alone other expenses. The first external audit, once that finally happened after a lot of blocking attempts by Zhou, concluded output was already below 60 per cent capacity. It was the worst management I've ever seen.

In his late fifties, Zhou was the most uneducated and belligerent person you could imagine. Endlessly spitting. Not that I don't spit myself, you know, now and again, but he was so crass about it, he would even phlegm up in crowded elevators or during meals. He had extremely oily hair, probably from smoking constantly, and was often absent from the office for lunches with his connections. Living proof of what I often heard said in the province, around the country for that matter, that top state-owned enterprise people were political appointments, not commercially-savvy people like they claimed.

Weirdly, though, instead of questioning Zhou's participation a strange denial gripped the situation.

The other players ignored his bad management. Instead there was a surreal concentration on vague, verbal, plans for joint improvements and more open communications.

In the first biannual review I raised concerns at Zhou's excessive use of company money for banquets and other entertainment, which included prostitutes though I didn't mention that, but I did write about the large numbers of gifts for officials and business connections, Party members and many others. He must have been going through several thousand US dollars weekly which was not something an American investor would tolerate. Nobody seemed to care and that part of the report was finally cut, or certainly toned down a lot.

Players were also unconcerned about Mr Lu even though he controlled 13.5 per cent and was hardly better than Zhou.

I had already raised questions about Lu's family interests in manufacturing computer parts. They weren't direct competitors. But it was noticeable that Lu seemed intrigued by operational knowledge and unconcerned about quality management or profitability.

At least Lu was usually in the office. Representatives from the Shanghai consortium, on the other hand, slept from the outset, rarely attended meetings and were seemingly unmoved by Zhou's poor performance or Lu's pilfering.

Considering all this it was inevitable there would be a default on repayments soon enough. When it happened, Zhou scandalously used a junior staff member to verbally inform our side; it must have been about eighteen months into the contract. You get used to things like that in China and I thought it was only a tactic to extend the repayment schedule.

But it was not.

I was completely amazed when Zhou, with Lu and the Shanghainese consortium as partners, switched ownership of the factory into a new holding. Urgent calls for meeting and consultations were evaded, Zhou pretending that nothing had happened.

Only by accident did I learn from informal contacts in Shanghai that new stakes had emerged in roughly similar proportions, only minus the Americans. The provincial government's stake had jumped to 25 per cent; Mr Lu became 27.5 per cent and the Shanghainese Consortium reached 45 per cent. An assortment of new names accounted for the other few per cent, none previously known to me, but probably they were Zhou's or Lu's family members, or other close connections.

Our contracts, our millions, had been lost to a shell, a ghost retaining not one single cent of our invested millions. Basically a collective middle finger had been raised: 'Hey guys, do what you fucking want! We've transferred ownership and you can't recover your money. We control the authorities, we *are* the law, and we're keeping your money!'

Zhou started a more active intimidation of the factory workers, seeking to frighten 'the foreigners', as both the Americans and us had become, with threats and challenges about strikes. Boasts about close connections with government and police amplified, and I noticed that many more local officials in green uniforms started to visit the factory. Zhou openly thanked them for 'protecting the people' when chances arose.

Then came the icing on the cake.

Zhou ceased production for the Americans and contracted with Lu's family-owned company to make similar keyboard casings.

Within weeks of switching ownership he was using our money, our investment, our factory and the Americans' know-how to do business with a competitor.

Hopes for a sensible resolution had died by then, and we stared investigating Zhou and Lu as we should have done to begin with. . . .

We soon discovered how little was known.

Public documentation was a nightmare. Foreigners couldn't source even basic records from the equivalent of Companies House. Confirming simple facts like Zhou's home address seemed impossible. People could see we were getting impatient and used it against us.

The little information available was extremely hard to find.

Instead of costing US$250 and taking a few hours, like in the States, it cost over US$10,000 and took months of meetings and persuasion and sweeteners to get even near an answer. Near, that is, in the way New York is nearer to California than it is to the moon. I'm sure we infringed the Foreign Corrupt Practices Act plenty.

The province was riddled with bureaux and departments that people with good connections like Zhou or Lu could ignore. Foreigners like us, no matter that we were ethnic Chinese, had to trudge through them all, bounced from one to another. Someone said during all of this: 'You may be ethnic Chinese, but you're still American.'

I developed Kafkaesque feelings about impenetrable bureaucracy. I know China can make you think like that, especially when everything seems to require dinners and banquets before meetings with underlings and then briefing mixed teams, but in the darker times the place felt like a realm of thieves, a place where the dignity of office and law . . . well, it was just meaningless.

Thankfully the Americans shared documents and contracts, an openness of day versus night compared to Mr Zhou and his cronies.

Eventually, and this whole legal process expanded over a year or more, we learned the full details about the Shanghai Consortium. Zhou's identity also became clearer. When a British bank based in Hong Kong published an investors' warning on Mr Lu and his family firm, effectively assassinating his credibility with reports about, shall we say, a copyright-infringing product, we felt encouraged.

Sensing our closeness Zhou and Lu started to use nationalism as a weapon.

They went back to the factory and demanded the workers hold fast in 'controlling destinies over foreigners'. Claims of persecution by 'unsympathetic powers' followed. Zhou stirring things with Jiang Ze Min thought quotations, shouting loudly that the foreign devils wanted to make the Motherland lose face and were plotting to Westernise and divide people.

Bare-faced lies, of course, especially the claims that low investment by us and demanding conditions had caused the production problems, when it was his mismanagement from day one. It was also really sickening to hear his talk about foreign powers never being the underdog. After a few months of that I openly replied that it's easy to lose face when you begin with two.

Lawyers in Hong Kong eventually resolved some matters through courts in the territory, where the loan had been covenanted. We had unsuccessfully tried provincial courts and I would not recommend them to *anyone.*

The Hong Kong ruling was a turning point.

It extracted from the provincial government verbal assurances our money would be 'honoured', they carefully avoided 'returned'. Zhou would 'be imprisoned and punished', though we never found out for how long or where. It seemed unlikely he would be properly punished when the Party's local newspaper wrote he had been 'led astray by drink, sex, and the decadent life of exploiting countries'. I honestly think Zhou was parachuted in to another state-owned enterprise or joint venture.

Still, the important thing was that Zhou disappeared and, surprisingly, our money re-appeared, though minus ten per cent which to this day nobody can explain.

Lu disappeared shortly afterwards but that's a whole other story I won't go into. . . .

Around that time, national laws were relaxed to allow the Americans majority ownership, which they achieved by purchasing our stake for around US$5 million. Frankly we were lucky to get even that given the poor state of the factory. The provincial government insisted on retaining a 12.5 per cent stake, which I'm sure the Americans would have preferred to avoid. They were desperate to become a 'woofie', a Wholly Foreign-Owned Enterprise.

Losing US$7 million with nothing to show except headaches is a very expensive lesson, embarrassing too. The Japanese bank on whose behalf I made the loan may yet sue, maybe not, that's unclear.

Fortunately they can't point many fingers given their mediocre returns. They've lost a ton of money in China, Asia too, from poor investment decisions. If you want evidence that handshakes and emotional-based decisions *never* beat sound commercial calculation then Japanese banks are probably that proof.

My biggest mistake was over-emotionalising association with the famous American company, the one owning 49 per cent, and under-documenting the Chinese side, which in the end controlled 51 per cent. Looking back it seems an elementary mistake. You simply must monitor who is what, who has what, and who does what. It's critical. A simple 'Mr Zhou, CEO', which we tolerated initially, is inadequate and hopeless, and probably suicidal.

I should have prepared a file with names and addresses of judges and police and other external authorities to consult during problems. I should have met them too, or people in our management team, and I'm sure Zhou would have been less manipulative and abusive if that happened.

We thought involving commercial arms of the government would make things clean, or cleaner. But they are easily tempted to protect their interests proactively, and illegally, for example by withholding company data.

We should have been wary, too, of delegating recruitment to local partners.

We left that to Zhou's team and learned the hard way that local partners, given half a chance, recruit cronies, often expensively and rarely productively. I can tell you that new blood like that gravitates towards dubious privileges like flies onto shit.

Auditing, too, must be tighter than we were.

In a way the Americans tempted fate, both theirs and ours, by reducing financial due diligence to twice-a-year. That's something never seen in the States; it would have been quarterly, even monthly at the beginning. Zhou became very practised at excuses like 'It's a bad time' or 'We're busy', and they were often clueless about the factory's true performance.

We also should have audited with foreign accountants. They're more neutral and their families can't be leveraged during problems.

This experience was very expensive. True. And it was very emotionally draining for me.

But in China's defence I would note that comparable struggles in Indonesia or Thailand can be much more violent. Vietnam, too, has many more physical encounters. Not that there is zero violence. I have seen worrying stuff in this province and other places. But in south-east Asia locals can more easily force police investigations and encourage them to be violent too.

On a personal note this terrible time also made me see how important speaking Putonghua is, and studying Chinese philosophy and culture too. Efforts in this area help you play on ideas and ideals of justice and honour and reciprocity.

And these, I believe, will help me create decent information about business partners in future. Despite the loss of so much money, I'm more optimistic than before, which probably sounds strange. Perhaps it's because I still love the country. I do love China. Though it helps that it wasn't really my money.

*   *   *

KWOK-YA, male entrepreneur, 44

Hong Kong Special Administrative Region, southern China

'Never assume you'll extract honesty from famous people: even billionaires, the Queen of England or some other King of the Universe can trick you when trouble happens.'

VEHICLE TUNING AND MAINTENANCE was profitable in Hong Kong during the eighties.

Start-up investment was high but we planned to target fleets of taxis and minibuses, which always needed regular engine maintenance and oil changes. Wheel balancing was also a growing area. Despite high costs we felt confident because of good connections with a car cleaning business. It also looked possible to win some Hong Kong Government business, including police motorcycles.

Sino-Zenith, a well-known vehicle importer, invested 22.5 per cent. A young mechanic called Tony, who knew cars and engine tuning well, showed his commitment by investing another 22.5 per cent. The controlling interest of 55 per cent was divided equally between myself and Mr Lok, or I should say that was our verbal agreement over dinner. I still remember his enthusiasm at a prosperous future.

But not quite!

Kin-Lok's daughter came to my apartment the following weekend and delivered strong praise of her father. 'So great,' she explained, 'so honest' and 'so well thought of in the community.' He would respect my independence in future cooperation. Operating decisions would be mine alone, and she had lots of other assurances too. Each ended at the same point: 'Someone so famous would never, could never, cheat people.'

She wanted my agreement to a 51:49 split in our share, with the larger and controlling part for her father.

Well, after such a speech, I was convinced there weren't any daggers in her smiles. In fact there was casualness in her words, innocence even, and I signed the next day.

You need to understand I was inexperienced in those days, in my thirties and yet to establish as a successful entrepreneur. It was clear that I would still run the business day-to-day and one per cent mattered little.

My family also thought this was acceptable. Mr Lok was a senior figure in Hong Kong politics. My mother was very impressed with his steely grey hair and what she called 'senior figure presence'. Papa also spoke positively. He liked his pro-business speeches in one of the elected bodies, I won't mention which one but he saw Mr Lok's frequent interviews on television. My parents were very traditional in some matters, and believed the senior Mr Lok would behave honestly and decently.

It soon became clear that Mr Lok would not meddle in operations. He hardly did a thing. But this was far from the entire picture.

He expected face constantly, expressed most obviously, frequently, in *ad hoc* payments. These were possible because he was not paid a salary but with his majority position, the one I signed over, he could charge and receive expense payments on his own signature.

Even if he turned up briefly for a coffee to discuss work, however briefly, he billed for time. Attending a chamber of commerce conference? That was strictly all-expenses paid. Reviewing new contracts? Consultancy fees. Marketing campaigns where he gave his personal endorsement he called professional services, that was his favourite term.

Free-of-charge servicing for his three cars, plus those of his friends and connections, was also expected and also became a steady commitment.

On our first anniversary he even sent a decorator's bill for his personal flat. 'Entertaining for business development', he wrote, which made me suspicious because the decorating firm was run by one of his friends.

People started talking.

Tony, the young mechanic, would say of Kin-Lok: 'If the mat is not straight, our Master won't sit.' Everything was highly ritualised and we had to respect him with silence. I think that was when I allowed myself thoughts that Kin-Lok had planned to capture the company from the start and use it to pay for some of his high life.

Then he wanted an office: 'Any Chairman needs a prominent and respectful location to build relations.'

We had little space. There was 6,000 square feet for operations. But he grabbed over 700 square feet for his office. That appeared, frankly, more bizarre than the decorator's bill. Few families have an apartment so large, let alone an office for a single person. My own small room had no outside view, only a window overlooking the workshop.

His new office sign was also extravagant. Our company name was pushed to the right corner whilst Kin Lok's full name, plus his various political titles, were so prominent I'm sure a sparrow could read them from Kowloon; a passenger could have read them from an aeroplane.

People started more than just talking.

Willingness to believe that provided business did well it wasn't our business how Mr Lok promoted himself was fading.

Then came his daughter and all patience started to wash away. Leaving a good job in investment banking to work as her father's assistant seemed odd, right from the start. Even though Kin-Lok carefully reminded everyone that his daughter was paid from his political allowances, not by our company, people weren't happy. They became confused why she sometimes worked 'for us' and at other times Kin-Lok would say she worked 'with us'.

Sheung Wan was also quite far away from his government offices in Central too, so something was a bit suspicious.

Tony heard rumours that Kin-Lok was claiming HK$80,000 each month from one government body and another HK$150,000 from another public source, both for the same thing: employing assistants and running his office. Relations worsened when she tried to influence working processes on the shop-floor, but that's another story.

Tension was rising and rising and Sino-Zenith initiated a private meeting to discuss Kin-Lok's expenses and 'crooked practices'. They supported the business overall, by then it was making quite good progress, but were concerned at the variety and extent of Mr Lok's expenses, which were approaching twenty per cent of our outgoings. I did not share the rumours about his daughter, why make a problem worse I thought, but hoped for better cooperation and more open communications. The Sino-Zenith boss nodded but I could tell he was not happy.

A couple of hours afterwards he telephoned to remind me of something that he hadn't want to say to my face but was in his heart: 'A businessman should look at things simply and straightforwardly,' he paused to let me agree. 'What is put in should be received.'

That message was much clearer than before. He disliked Kin Lok's tricks over expenses and it was my responsibility to prevent them.

Coincidentally we were buying new equipment. Costing a few million dollars, the British supplier required a letter of credit before delivery. Our bank required personal guarantees for this letter, with which I had no problem. Likewise the boss of Sino-Zenith and Tony the mechanic signed. But Mr Lok, our major shareholder, would not.

His refusal threw *everyone* into total disbelief.

He had most influence. He was happy to prominently display his name above our workshop. And he repeatedly claimed dubious expenses. Yet he would *not* sign a personal letter of credit for a vital step in our operations.

Eventually the boss of Sino-Zenith arranged a second letter of credit but his patience was as dead as Genghis Khan.

When the *coup d'état* unfolded Kin-Lok was told: 'Resign or leave by other methods'.

Arrangements were made to refuse any more expense claims and my secretary quietly collected the cheque book and company chop from his office whilst he and his daughter were out. Returning to changed locks must have been quite shocking. He was face-conscious and I don't think anyone ever treated him like that.

He immediately committed to reducing expenses and moving his daughter away. It was a kind of apology, I suppose, an admission of guilt but it was too late. Even when he offered a letter of credit to *me,* not the bank of course, I refused the insult on behalf of the company.

Following Kin-Lok's resignation Sino-Zenith took 51 per cent and suddenly I was in partnership with a listed company and relieved to have ended conflict with Kin-Lok in a single stroke.

But Mr Lok's anticipation was like a hare with three escape entrances to its burrow. He had transferred a lot of profits a few days before being fired; he must have sensed problems. Despite an action in the civil courts we never saw that money again.

Then came the poisoned letters, over two thousand of them, which he sent to customers and prominent people in Hong Kong and Shenzen, where we had set up a related operation.

They were the most amazing and distressing lies. I still meet people who remember them. The words may have been polite but many suspected I had done something quite bad . . . and I have had to live with a lot of hate. I still haven't recovered from all those feelings.

I responded with my own letter.

But Lok increased the stakes with a full-size advertisement in large English and Chinese newspapers, including *Ming Pao* and the *South China Morning Post*. In the same issue a journalist wrote about his business successes, including his strong reputation for honesty. Replacing more of my beams with rotten timber, a second article the following month described how he had left the industry due to inefficient business partners. It was about me again. . . .

I definitely had no idea how to respond which worried me greatly. Even Sino-Zenith were starting to have bad thoughts about me, but with no connections to help me make an effective and public reply I had to accept my bad fate.

It is a few years on now and Lok still hates me, definitely his daughter does, and they must both hate that the business grew after they left. He must have been beside himself when an American company bought us out and we signed a deal with a huge bus fleet operator. . . .

Sometimes I ask for repayment of the stolen profits.

Not that I really need the money, it's only a point of justice for the harm he caused, but he grows angry and shouts that the matter is concluded according to the courts. It's like I am a disrespectful child, trying to steal from the parent, and he uses rude words that you certainly won't hear in his television interviews.

I have learnt that kowtowing to prestige can be a possibly fatal business decision.

Kin-Lok knew how important one tiny per cent was. I didn't. Let me tell you, I have *never* signed away control of any venture since then.

I tell my kids that someone beguiling and convincing in the public eye can easily be cheating in private. Influential and famous people can manipulate weaker partners, and quite skilfully too. Sending his daughter to my home was also the mark of a crafty operator. It implied an unimportant detail, when he knew it was the opposite. Never assume you will extract honesty from famous people: even billionaires, the Queen of England or some other King of the Universe can promise great business but trick you when trouble happens.

Famous people, in fact, are more likely to take advantage of ordinary people. That which succeeds they call their success and, when things go wrong, they retreat to what they know best, which is PR and image management. After they start rumours *nobody* will trust your side of things.

*   *   *

XIN-QUAN, female expatriate, 37

Guangdong Province, southern China

'Taking punch after punch in my arms and body all I remember was screaming: "What do you want? What do you want?"'

IT EXCITED ME in the way you expect when working abroad for the first time: adventure, cultural encounters, career development, travel opportunities, money. Three years in Guangdong Province seemed perfect in every way.

Other colleagues from Europe had not done very well and management hoped my roots would help.

When my husband was made redundant and an international school, King George V in Hong Kong, accepted our two girls, we decided to take the chance and arrived in the autumn that year.

I was to manage the recruitment and training of a second factory shift that would work from 4pm until midnight.

Our company's market share was approaching 20 per cent in some segments and the plan was for 25 per cent share within five years. That was only achievable with the extra output from two shifts. Helping to command a quarter of the biggest truck market in the world is still probably the most exciting project I've worked on. The people in headquarters sometimes called it 'the great fight'. You don't get that scale in Europe.

The first problem was quality standards in the factory, which was located to the west of Guangzhou. They were amazingly low.

Even senior staff arrived whenever they wanted apparently, and few on the factory floor washed equipment or uniforms regularly. Generally everyone and everything looked unprofessional and dirty, I mean *really* dirty, and the assembly line frequently seemed like anarchy. Men wandered through safety exclusion zones and left dirty tools scattered randomly. Others openly stole supplies. I remember being shocked to see cigarettes lit within spitting distance of petrol storage tanks. How there wasn't an explosion I have no idea.

Even though many lingered long after their shift ended, productivity was awful.

Factories in Europe can be bad but, to this day, I have never seen anything like it; it was surreal.

My first mistake, the most stupid looking back, was retaining the previous head of recruitment, Mr Yip.

A clean break would have been better. Remoulding habits and relations with traditional people like him are very difficult. I see that now. But I kept him as my deputy and gently repeated, to him and others in his former empire, that the decision had been made and I would be the new boss. I should have seen that this only fomented Mr Yip's resentment and plotting. It didn't make him more cooperative, that's for sure. Just because he nodded didn't mean he agreed.

By and large he was unfriendly, especially to junior staff, and particularly harsh to others from different departments, which should not happen in HR departments. He rarely compromised on office procedures or day-to-day events but I did little, other than make friendly and accommodating suggestions, which were increasingly deflected.

I think it was inevitable, and my fault to some extent, that within a couple of months he felt confident enough to warn me in his broken English: 'I hope for good cooperation. Otherwise it can be difficult to be good to you by my alliances and me.' I smiled back. But I was deeply shocked at such an unmistakable threat.

It became obvious that Mr Yip's interpretation of 'good cooperation' meant he would select the second shift. This was the very opposite of HQ's wishes.

But what did I do?

I still can't believe it, it's actually embarrassing now, but again I stayed more or less silent and again I made a mistake. Something naïve inside me thought that a second chance might just prove HQ wrong.

Mr Yip, for his part, exploited my move and increasingly sent subordinates to deliver controversial messages verbally. He stopped putting things in writing. Again it was the time I should have stood up and acted.

Mr Yip's recommended actions for the second shift were highly suspicious.

Work experience was impossible to appraise realistically. Education, for example, was summarised, in both Chinese and English, as 'very good student' or 'ideal knowledge collection', omitting details of where and when they went to school or what they studied. Professional qualifications in mechanical engineering or metalwork were particularly vague; things like 'strongly qualified engineer' appeared. That was it! No dates, no specialisations, no experience, no nothing.

I finally changed my mind, what else could I do, reminding Mr Yip in writing that headquarters had engaged me to recruit staff. I wished to start afresh, and assume greater responsibility. I didn't say, outright, that I would direct everything, but he must have sensed my meaning.

Following re-opening of recruitment at local universities and other places of my choosing, Mr Yip became extremely unhappy. He let it be known that I had 'very disrespectfully' accused him of recruiting stooges or people in his family network or people who had bribed him. That I had done no such thing, though he probably was guilty of it, that I tried to stay polite and professional, counted for nothing.

Mr Yip's face grew longer each day and other childish repercussions followed: delays in correspondence; whispering campaigns; low-level disobedience. It was nothing specific I could complain about, but there was still a very noticeable attrition, bringing nothing to a head whilst leaving more and more things about my authority in question.

But I never thought our tension would become violent . . . which it did when the second wave of job applications were translated independently of Mr Yip and I denied him copies.

Three men came to my home one morning, shouting loudly after I opened the courtyard gate, having tricked their way in by enquiries about shopping deliveries. The biggest one slapped the back of my head, another kicked my calf, pushing me into a wall whilst the third punched my arm and stopped me from running away. It was well organised.

As they started to pound into me I worried that the choppers would soon emerge and I would bleed to death, my body discovered by Pierre and the girls.

And taking punch after punch all I remember was screaming in Putonghua: *'What do you want? What do you want?'*

I have never been so scared in my life. . . .

They slammed me over my car bonnet and demanded if I knew 'Manager Yip from the factory?'

When my acknowledgement calmed them, briefly, I remember a rush of relief, perhaps it was even a little happiness, that someone else wished to harm Mr Yip: Fire him? Demote him? Cause his family and friends problems?

But then they shouted in rehearsed English: 'Give Mr Yip respect to decide the new jobs!'

Which is when I knew. And as they battered me once more, this time around the face, I remember shouting back, tears mixing with anger: 'Okay! Okay!'

Disbelief also gave way to anger at headquarters back in Europe who became involved when pictures of my bruises were sent for the insurance claim. It was the first time any violence had happened to expatriate staff and even before the police investigation was complete — they never found the men who beat me — Mr Yip was dismissed and escorted from the factory. Despite explanations about 'bad connections acting without permission' and other obvious lies, his fate was sealed and I never saw him again in the factory.

Which is not to say Mr Yip disappeared from my life.

My personal security was upgraded. They hired two full-time drivers who had been policemen to accompany the family and me. 'In order to prevent further injuries,' the drivers sometimes said in broken English, which was a very worrying phrase to hear repeatedly.

Even after a week the constant escort was draining. Neither body-guard smiled much, becoming gloomy and unvarying reminders of the unspoken threat. Sometimes I felt them think it was my fault, a little at least. The rowdy foreigner not understanding local ways.

Meanwhile over 300 staff were recruited and trained within four months, incredibly, and that is still my best professional achievement. Unfortunately, though, profits did not increase. Revenues continued, yes, but larger distributors started to avoid payment more often.

Some would take delivery of trucks numbering in the dozens, hundreds sometimes, but encounter mystifying circumstances making it impossible to pay for everything, or even anything. If we valued the relationship prices must be reduced or we must be patient. Sometimes this can happen in Europe, but only in China will a famous and large company like ours tolerate that.

More worryingly, rumours circulated that Mr Yip was somehow involved in worsening the collection problems.

He had been seen banqueting with our valuable customers a few times. Whispers followed that the non-payments was a scheme of revenge aimed at me specifically and the company in general. People said he was creating fires and watching them burning.

Worries and tensions like that take their toll and after many destructive arguments and hate and lies by staff still loyal to Mr Yip that I won't describe, Mr Yip had his wish granted. I was invited, politely but clearly *invited,* to return home early.

Returning in circumstances like that . . . well . . . nobody was more disappointed than me.

In most regards my husband disliked Guangzhou, especially the steady conflict at work and the bodyguards. That would make it difficult for anyone to look on things positively, though he has a kind heart and loves the Chinese people. For that I am grateful and I love him very much.

I'm just thankful he was taking our daughters shopping during the assault. Pierre, I'm sure, would have tried to protect me physically and perhaps they would have killed him.

For myself, I suppose I will miss the country. In a way. It will always be my home.

And the experience did bring me closer to my mother, who came from Nanning in the south-east. I still use the Chinese name her father gave me, which I love because it means happy and beautiful. As Pierre says it does sound beautiful in a French accent . . . *Xin-Quan.*

For the children, well, I'm glad they saw their home country as they grew up, and that it existed for a time in their hearts and their world, as it is in their blood. They'll always feel it defines them in a special way, I hope. Unfortunately their experiences were also far from positive and they liked Hong Kong so much more than Guangzhou.

I still think about how foolish I was not to make a clean break with Mr Yip.

He showed me that some people can spend the rest of their days taking revenge, anything to recover their face. I should have broken down and cried when I fired him, no matter his bad deeds, and he might have left me alone, perhaps.

I still also have dreams about arguing back during the assault, perhaps describing Mr Yip as an idiot and a fool. I could have told his thugs to go to hell. . . .

But in real life it's not like that, is it?

I know that would have only caused more violence and the important thing is that I escaped without injury, it has to be when you've a family.

*   *   *

YUN-LIANG, female journalist, 38

Tianjin Municipality, northeast China near Beijing

'Authorities quickly revealed their knowledge of who we were, where we lived, what we did and what we advocated. They knew everything.'

I ALWAYS LOVED reporting big events and I'm sure that passion secured my job-exchange with the Hong Kong newspaper.

Mr Wen wanted me to learn modern techniques and help create a 'foreign country style'. As senior editor he planned new prosperity for our newspaper in Tianjin.

Caught up in the pre-1997 excitement Hong Kong offered a huge amount to learn and write about, and was quite shockingly free. I had never encountered such independence, it was amazing really, like working in the future.

Most official newspapers practised then, as they still do, strict adherence to Marxism, supporting the Party and 'correctly channelling public opinion'. But in Hong Kong political propaganda was embarrassing. Even Governor Patten could be criticised, right down to his taste in food. Uncritical political pieces, in fact, couldn't even get published, which was radically different from Tianjin where we had to be very cautious and respectful about leaders and important officials.

Sometimes I e-mailed Mr Wen with descriptions of Hong Kong politicians suffering loss of face, or stories about rich and influential people ridiculed despite having powerful connections. I thought that was exactly the 'foreign country style' he wanted, but he never replied, which I suppose should have told me what his true heart felt. Instead I assumed he was like some older and traditional men that rarely responded to junior people.

Leaving Hong Kong and its climate of criticism, the nightlife too, was not easy and I still miss the city.

Even though I was promoted on the Tianjin News Events Desk, helping Mr Wen supervise staff, it was disappointing that we never really discussed Hong Kong. My insights to 'foreign country style' counted for little and attempts to start discussions met with blank faces. After a time I got the message to keep quiet until further notice.

Mr Wen was, however, happy to see trivial pieces about asking directions in English and how to haggle over prices in US dollars.

'What happened to Hong Kong-style criticism of leaders?' I once asked, but was decisively reminded to think about other ideas that help the people.

A few months later Mr Wen sent me with a photographer to review the sacking of state workers in the Bohai Gulf area.

Street protests had apparently become very angry, it was rumoured that several thousand workers were demanding unpaid salary. Trials of dishonest and incompetent officials had also been demanded.

I was a bit surprised he sent me, but to Mr Wen it was a minor story and I don't think he recognised how much it would appeal to me. If he had I don't think he would have sent me. I only remember his cautious and unsmiling detachment as we left for the station: Only simple facts, he stressed. The only reason for investigation was the nearness to Beijing; the 'centre-of-the-centre', he sometimes called the capital, or when he was feeling poetic 'the source of clouds and the winds'. You only know how much power you don't have when you see Beijing, he told me once.

As requested my first article covered a routine meeting between workers' representatives and their former managers. I listed plans for future protests over Zhou Ming-xin, a leader arrested in the early days of the tension. It was the kind of neutral and sleepy material that Mr Wen wanted.

But the story grew.

Police actions created only bigger protests and city leaders sent for army units to smash the demonstration, which was done very aggressively with teargas and baton charges and other violent tactics. Thirty more workers were arrested, that we could count, and it was suddenly a great time to be a journalist, with a magnificent story on your hands and photographs to match. Perhaps it might even become a classic conflict like 1989, I thought to myself. . . .

I telephoned Mr Wen to ask for another week of investigation.

His permission, given quite reluctantly, was for only two more days. But no more. 'Only basic information is required,' he repeated and hung up rudely. *Fuck your mother's ancestors,* I remember whispering to the disconnected phone.

Back in the troubled city, hundreds of workers, perhaps thousands, were concentrating to demand the release of those already arrested.

As we interviewed Zhou's elderly wife she too was arrested, police overpowering her and another worker in the small street who tried to intervene. It seemed whenever anyone was arrested we captured it on film. I e-mailed a second article to Wen with pictures.

Wen finally lost patience, demanding our immediate return in another rude phone call.

I spent some final hours collecting names and addresses of workers who had been arrested, especially ones for 'illegal demonstrations in public places', which the authorities often used for more serious punishments.

Minutes before we boarded the train news leaked that Mr Zhou had been taken to hospital in a serious condition. I desperately wanted to visit the hospital because I was certain what that meant. But the photographer had a cooler head, a more political head anyway, and dragged me onboard with warnings not to upset Mr Wen.

Drafting a third article as we journeyed back to Tianjin, I detailed rumours that Zhou's ill-health was due to torture, not old age as the authorities claimed, and contrasted the policing style with the restraint of Hong Kong. It had the makings of an unforgettable series of stories, and I was sure Wen would print them and send us back for more.

Wen, in fact, was angry at my personal waste of time and money: 'Your reports are counter-state,' he observed coolly and put them in his drawer. 'We are better than Hong Kong journalists or the BBC or CNN. Remember Mao! Always be modest and avoid great-power chauvinism resolutely. . . .'

When I quietly pointed out that I wasn't being a chauvinist, as far as I could tell, or seeking to grab power, but simply being a good reporter Wen shouted that his decision was made. My type of anti-state coverage *must* stop.

By the end of that week, a junior staff member came to tell me that Wen wished me to change jobs and start monitoring general trends via the Internet.

He knew that success stories about highways and science parks and other mind-numbing things would drive me crazy. I'm sure he wanted me to leave so he could criticise the polluting effects of Hong Kong to his Party cronies.

Even simple stories about sandstorms near Beijing, or dried up rivers further north in the Jilin area, were rejected: *Unnecessarily controversial.* Travel outside the city was consistently denied: *Unnecessary for work purposes.*

But I refused to resign. I suspected that Wen would make getting another journalism job in the city unlikely and I wasn't about to fall into his trap. My parents taught me well.

Bored at work, trapped in front of a computer like a fly on flypaper, I began investigating why authorities thought the Internet was being used for counter-state purposes. What else was there to do?

When a website that I was monitoring posted details about the eight-year sentence given to Zhou for 'downloading counter-state materials from the Internet', my interest in the old Bohai Gulf story returned. I submitted a piece about the sentence, the longest for Internet-related activities, because I was certain Zhou had done no such thing; his wife said her husband couldn't even *operate* a computer.

Something in me decided to add the protests had been fuelled by information circulating via Internet cafés: *A relevant and important national trend,* I wrote.

When Wen killed the copy instantly, ignoring my looks and scowling at me for days afterwards, I only became more determined.

I submitted a second story about an adjustment of Zhou's punishment. A senior judge had looked at the case and claimed Zhou was also guilty of subverting state power by spreading reactionary materials; he therefore deserved a longer sentence, eventually set at an amazing ten years.

Wen lost his patience and delivered a loud lecture to all staff: 'The Party requires journalists to *strictly* avoid sensitive issues like Taiwan, separatist Uygur movements in Xinjiang or Tibet, and extremist cults. . . .' He couldn't bring himself to say Falun Gong, but everybody knew, and I'm sure everyone could also sense, this was about me and my Hong Kong ways. 'Never forget the "Golden Rule" of speaking positively and avoiding controversy. Stability is our central principle.'

I think it was the way he said it, so patriarchal, as if we were children, and I finally decided to fight.

Secret investigations in Internet chat rooms followed. Their open sharing of information represented exactly what Wen was against, and exactly what impressed me in Hong Kong.

Investigation had its risks.

Wen had placed on the notice board after his 'Golden Rule' speech, a government proclamation that chat-rooms were unreliable and unpatriotic sources of information. He carefully highlighted with a yellow pen their 'exceptionally bad record of delivering illegal messages'.

Disobedience to Wen, however, had become a habit and articles from *People's Daily* weren't about to stop me.

I expanded my secret interests to monitor state offices that had cracked down on Internet use. As more people were arrested and more Internet sites banned I kept a list. From a journalistic point-of-view it was unproductive because only inconsequential and childish stories made it past Wen. But it felt *good*. Wen and what he stood for had become my enemy and I started to express this feeling by meeting like-minded rebels.

I helped write secret letters in English to important people in the United States and other nations, encouraging them to campaign for a free Internet in China.

I arranged cooperation with a Hong Kong-based website listing people wrongly or suspiciously imprisoned.

A central government threatened by exchanges of opinions was a bad sign, I wrote in an anonymous article. Banning ideas just for hinting at overthrowing state power or toppling the socialist system, or abstract ideas like 'destroying national unity', is unfair. These freedoms had been allowed in Hong Kong before 1997, I concluded, which was very successful in those days.

We became involved with campaigns at universities for students to use anonymous proxy services, avoiding blocks on sensitive web pages by security forces.

Perhaps I had been safe up to then, but temptation overwhelmed me like opium.

I submitted a story describing how history showed China must reach out to young people with more than punishments and secret monitoring. Sharing of information in the Internet age requires mutual trust and a more open society, I wrote. I criticised those who preferred to imitate the past rather than create the future. In short, it was everything that Wen stood against.

. . . the arrests came at night. . . .

Authorities quickly revealed their knowledge of who we were, and where we lived, and what we did, and what we advocated. They knew everything.

Questioned for a whole day I finally collapsed, exhausted and hungry. *Guilty as the people charge.*

After sentencing later that week we were led off, elbows bound behind our back like common criminals, and I glimpsed Wen in the crowd. His face, mocking and full of pride, told me that he *had* sold us out, he *had* always known, he *had* monitored me, he *had* made me pay for disloyalty.

Thankfully, because of the people's investment in my training in Hong Kong, I received only a one year sentence and was released after eighteen months. The extra six months were a gift from the deputy prison governor: *To continue my education about state rights,* one of the warders told me.

Others were less fortunate.

Bai, the leader of our efforts, was sentenced for downloading pro-democracy material. Even though he used a computer in his private house they claimed he was 'carrying materials in a public place', which turned out to be the train station where they arrested him. When he received five years he started crying, louder when his old friend Shen got seven years for publishing subversive articles on the Internet, which was a guide to free e-mail sites in the United States. Dr Tang, an academic at a Normal University, whose record of protest dated back to the Anti-Bourgeois Liberalisation of the seventies when he was a student in America, received three years for spreading information about riots. Professor He of the mechanical engineering department received four years for helping him. His wife got three years for cooperating with her husband. Another graduate student was told he must be in prison for a minimum of two years for 'generally supporting the criminals'.

Fortunately prison wasn't completely bad. I was not badly assaulted often.

Some inmates even said I was an intellectual in a positive sense, having a patriotic future in my heart. That's pleasing to hear when you feel destroyed just for trying to help the country.

I became good friends with a university lecturer. 'Your mistake,' he told me, 'Was not appreciating change in others. Simply because Mr Wen wanted Hong Kong-style journalism at one time, he may have changed his mind. Perhaps he was forced by political forces, or by his boss. Perhaps even you misunderstood his original idea?'

In my bad days, when I shouted that Wen was as spineless as a bowl of noodles, he calmed me.

On release from prison one of Wen's editors sent me a message not to revisit the newspaper. I had attacked state institutions and was considered a 'dangerous anti-state element'.

Eventually I ended up in Shanghai and found work as a translator. I still have to visit the police, occasionally they visit me, and explain my life events and Internet activities. But my husband forgives the interruptions. It avoids trouble in the long-term.

As you can imagine I have no respect for Wen and how he played his cards. What a low person. First sending me to Hong Kong to learn foreign ways, then changing his mind but not telling me, even when I was in imminent danger of arrest. What decency is that?

Avoiding conflict with cunning people is about reading the silence. At times lack of noise can be as threatening and damaging as real noise. Simply because people said one thing at one time doesn't mean you can trust them forever.

They have a good saying in Shanghai: *A rock is unmoved by wind,* the wise are unaffected by either blame or credit from others. That's my feeling these days. Don't depend on others . . . which I suppose is what Mr Wen taught me in his deceitful and silent way.

*   *   *

SIMON, male equities broker, 42

Hong Kong Special Administrative Region, southern China

'It was my first serious warning that Julian was a nasty piece of work, frankly a blatant liar who felt neither guilt nor concern at racism.'

I HAD LEFT my previous job eager to become more ethical and earn money in a decent way.

But several years of slog had proven that wouldn't work, at any rate in the short-term, and with a wife and family to support and savings to revive I had to return to employment. No choices.

I promised myself, however, to stay different. There would be no lying, no constant looking to my left-brain, and I would prove in a nine-to-five setting that honesty in Hong Kong broking can work, even if I had to work for another house to make the point.

Briefly I had met Julian years before, a reflection of the small expatriate circles that characterise Hong Kong.

It was when arranging some dancing girls for a stag party, that was something I did in those days before I was married. Julian was the best man and my girls had stripped to wild applause. Let's just say nakedness and strawberries and cucumbers, you get the idea. But afterwards it had become rather complicated.

Not only did Julian fail to keep the club sweet, although I admit one of my classic memories of Hong Kong was being frog-marched with semi-naked girls through a room of super-rich diners. But he also failed to deliver the cash. After chasing and chasing with no success, I remember taping three sheets of A4 paper together and faxing a repeating loop, each saying in massive letters: GIVE US OUR MONEY OR WE'LL SUE. FROM YOUR TARTS. You'll sense that he had made me rather angry by then. . . .

But it worked.

Julian called early the next morning, rather agitated because his secretary had been shocked at fifty-odd pages of the same rude fax, which I found hilarious. The money arrived by messenger and in cash by lunchtime.

He had forgotten that little event, we had only actually met for a few drunken minutes, but you could definitely say it all revealed his character.

His broking operation was divided so that the largest team sold to multinational enterprises, the MNEs. A second and smaller team targeted large local businesses and a few others, including myself, handled the SMEs, small-to-medium sized enterprises.

Which was a toughie: even though plentiful the SMEs made up by far the smallest sector in sales value, probably a tenth of the MNE sector, and serious prospects were very difficult to find.

From the start it was clear Julian's management style hinged on explicit threats about rivals entering your sector if your sales dipped, regardless of market performance. Your loss probably meant someone else's gain; it was that kind of very aggressive broking management.

Amiable and relaxed about office hours during my recruitment, Julian quickly became abrupt and aggressive in insisting that sixty or more hours per week in the office was expected, whether or not I endured fifteen-odd hours of commuting. 'Whatever it said in the contract.'

Nor did Julian care that I didn't really fit in with the other brokers.

Most were Canadian or Australian, the house was headquartered in Toronto of all places, and as a Brit I never felt completely welcome. The worst of it was the undercurrents of racism and sexism that Julian tolerated and, I began to sense, encouraged.

Up-market, high-pressure and thirty-something testosterone-laden boys can behave like that, I knew that, broking is about that. But I found it incredibly offensive to see Julian, the boss let's remember, disrespecting Chinese so badly. Openly he would describe them as 'stupid local bastards'. Out of earshot, or so he thought, he'd call them 'useless effing chinks'. Singaporeans were bananas, because they were yellow on the outside but white inside. Indians were 'effing smelly janglies' or 'arse singers', after the Cantonese insult for Indians, many of whom are surnamed Singh.

I hated that racism. Terribly out of place in Hong Kong's relatively tolerant culture and it soon made me conflicted being in the same room, forced into silent acquiescence, and hating it, just hating it.

After a few months Julian fired a junior broker for allegedly stealing some files and other paperwork.

'That effing wanker! Thief and a liar!' he screamed around the office. More discreetly he added 'all they do is steal. Effing thieves!

And they're liars too. We're going to sue him! We're going to take his house away. We will!'

It was a great over-reaction, of course, and my first serious warning about the man I was involved with professionally, that by nature Julian was a nasty piece of work.

I'm sure Julian, for his part, sensed my personal distaste and he started to watch me more closely, governing the mood between us. If he was grumpy, then I kept my head down. If he was happier I could relax a little, but not a great deal.

As months passed his business decisions discouraged me. Even though the SME market was declining, it had boomed pre-1997 but never really recovered, Julian was still adamant at its resurrection. Yet when several months brought only modest returns compared to the MNEs, hardly surprising, he changed his mind, re-channelling my efforts into a small niche of the MNE market. Of course that's where I should have been to start with.

My distaste for Julian's 'management by measurement' approach strengthened appreciably, especially concerning his pet metric of at least three telephone hours a day. Bizarrely he refused to count incoming calls and eventually during one of our team meetings I observed this was open to abuse. When Julian was away, I explained, people knew they wouldn't be monitored and called friends or family. If clients or prospects called the results were also obvious:

'Is that so-and-so?'

'Yes, I'm sorry but there's someone on the other line. Can I call you back?'

'Sure. . . .'

Of course nobody was on the other line, it was just a way of jacking up the out-going calls.

Julian said nothing in that meeting, but a few days later called me to his office and revealed he was 'personally offended' at some aspects of both my behaviour and my performance. Improvements were expected and, yes, his numbers board would continue.

At a later team meeting a few months later I pointed out another problem, this time caused by Julian's preference for recording potential sales.

'People exaggerate. They'll say anything, even if they're false trails or things they doubt will happen.' I quoted an example about such-and-such sales prospects being out of town, so I wouldn't have any numbers for a day or two, but Julian darted poisonous looks and said he would like to record things anyway.

I discreetly rolled my eyes. . . .

Later that week, perhaps getting back at me by attacking others, he was funny like that, Julian decided to shut the office on Christmas Eve. Everyone was to take a day from their leave balance, a sort of forced holiday. I questioned that, wanting to keep my days stacked up for the kids' summer holidays, but in response he told his secretary to check with the Labour Department and issue a memo. This claimed they could legally shut the office whenever they wished.

Unimpressed, I really felt compelled to discuss this with Julian and went to see him: 'Whilst I agree shutting the office is legal, it's not quite the same as taking the day out of people's leave.'

'We think it's legal,' was Julian's very curt reply. Very rude.

'Well, I checked and in Hong Kong you can only force leave with thirty days' warning, which hasn't happened.'

'In that case I would like all staff to sign a form requesting Christmas Eve be taken from their annual leave,' and he beckoned his secretary.

I didn't want to sign, but the consequences were too dire.

That was a bleak holiday season. Hong Kong was getting panned by the markets anyway, and Julian made life tenser, no matter the holiday mood. In the quiet time before New Year another broker was fired, and that ended up in a great compensation tussle with Julian.

If you've worked for over two years you *are* owed two-thirds of your latest monthly salary for every year worked, rounded to a certain maximum. It was all clear and legal but Julian went ballistic when I pointed this out.

'He was fired for lack of performance and had plenty of warning letters,' blah blah blah. It was Julian spouting out of his arse, again.

When he finally came for me, there was no subtlety about it and I still recall some of his words: 'You're an effing c-word and you take the piss all the time.'

A written warning followed in a fortnight, an e-mail copied to his secretary which rather said it all about his manners, accompanied by a further ear-bashing over my pipeline numbers, the deals in hand. I quietly repeated my belief that there was no need for bullshit.

He called me to his office. By then my goal was keeping the job so I let him rant and scream, head bowed like a schoolboy, and slowly his energy ebbed. Retreating to my seat, the other staff offered little sympathy, subtly hinting I should know the game and then making arrangements for that night's drinks without inviting me.

They thought I was a prick, probably, but I felt more mature, more sensitive, more aware of our rights as employees, and more honest about our work. Frankly, I was pissed off enough to pick up a chair and bash in Julian's face, a few others too.

But I couldn't, I needed the job, that same old reason.

I couldn't face the bus home that day and had several beers by myself, well more than several, finally taking a taxi home, blowing money I should be saving for the kids. I remember crying into the window before falling into a deep sleep, drunkenly deep, and in the end the poor driver had to take me, Mr Comatose, to a police station where a friendly constable somehow discovered my identity. It was funny later, quite a bit actually, but at the time it only made me hate more what I was doing to myself, and Julian and his values more as well.

By the spring I felt certain it was only a matter of time before I would be fired.

Surprisingly, though, Julian spared me and instead fired two other brokers. I watched the whole procedure with interest: called into Julian's office; given the bad news; personally escorted by Julian to their desks; ushered out of the office by security staff, entry codes changed there and then. At least it was quick.

Longer lasting, though, were Julian's obligatory insults to the dearly departed.

They became, initially, either 'a wanker' or 'an arsehole' or 'a prick' or 'a dickhead'. Something offensive. And later he might add in racist epithets if they worked, which I won't repeat because they were so disgusting. And once he found an epithet he constantly repeated it. Even ex-clients could become 'rich so-and-so arseholes'; it was really bad stuff.

When my termination came I felt relieved, to tell the truth, having grown to hate the whole situation, and with it something of myself for being part of Julian's racism. I was having a quiet beer with my severance cheque by 3pm, wondering just how Julian would be insulting me to the others, and how they might be reacting.

I don't miss the near-daily clashes, though I would concede I miss the money.

It's bloody hard to be a white broker in Hong Kong at the moment. Even if you speak Cantonese, have a local wife and are educating your kids locally, some people avoid business with you.

But I would rather that struggle than the struggle of working for a racist, hate-filled, micro-manager *gweilo* like Julian.

Not to sound like an old man, but Julian taught me that foreign salesman and traders in Hong Kong can think lies, deceit and many other shocking tactics, are acceptable, provided you make your sale. Perhaps they sleep at night because they're not door-to-door selling dodgy vacuum cleaners to housewives in Surrey who don't need them. Perhaps they like lying. Who knows. Who effing cares.

I don't want revenge, really, and if I saw Julian again I wouldn't say a great deal. Other than you're a lying, racist, bastard, that is.

the poor

By China's own admission, nearly one half of its population live on under US$2 per day and the poorest fifth share less than one-twentieth of the national income. Poverty and China are as intertwined as China and the Party, and will remain so for several decades at least.

AN-NENG, female farm worker, 27

Fujian Province, southeast China

'Added to borrowings from family and friends, she paid the RMB100,000 deposit to the snakeheads.'

MY COUSIN DECIDED to leave for America on her twenty-fifth birthday.

We had listened to Ling's stories about California ever since her first marriage failed.

Thankfully she managed to dig out some money from that bad husband before she ran away. Added to borrowings from family and friends, she paid the RMB100,000 deposit to the snakeheads. The rest would have to paid on landing but that only required two or maybe three years' work in their clothing factory. She would soon be making a lot of money and be free to marry an American passport holder.

I loaned her RMB10,000 from my savings. Although that had taken five years to bank I trusted Ling to repay with good interest because she would be in America and making real money.

After Ling disappeared nobody said anything publicly because the authorities had spies around town. But we all knew what had happened and had good thoughts for Ling.

Some were jealous because her opportunity was so much better than staying a farm worker; several of them were already making plans to try something similar.

The news of Ling's death only spread because there were television reports about dead bodies found in a container near San Francisco. Someone in our circle calculated that the ship must have left Fujian Province the weekend Ling disappeared.

When CCTV listed the names of people discovered dead and Ling was on the list I worried that our money had gone for ever.

Thankfully the misfortune was reported in American newspapers and authorities in Beijing became interested. Local officials were forced to act. Within a week they announced the arrest of the snakehead leading 'The San Francisco Crime', as they called it. They discovered a lot of money in his house which would be returned to the families of his victims.

The snakehead would also be severely punished by the provincial leaders for humiliating China in the eyes of foreigners.

A group of us put together evidence of our financial connection to Ling and went to the authorities. She had borrowed RMB200,000 in total we said, it was safer to exaggerate with these people, and we intended to do a lot of good with this money in our village so as to prevent such things happening again.

An officer was very willing to write down our details. The case would clarify in due course, she said, and we should follow events closely in Party newspapers.

A few months later someone surnamed Fu appeared in the highest provincial court. When he was sentenced to life imprisonment, plus confiscation of his money, he cried in court and asked for mercy. None of us thought he should get any mercy for what he had done to Ling.

But the anti-people-smuggling office suddenly changed their story. Journalists had confused everyone with false stories about the money; they now claimed the amount recovered from Fu and his group had actually been very small. Senior figures had calculated what was available and authorised payment of RMB8,888 per victim. But that was it.

Plus, to receive the money we had to sign a letter criticising the snakeheads theft of An-neng's money and say we understood the authorities had done their best to recover the full sum.

Our suspicions were raised but what could we do?

Who knows what senior figures had become involved.

For me the most shady aspect is that even the authorities abuse fleeing people. They are as bad as the snakeheads. The only difference is that they can't be accused or punished. No wonder people like Ling are an endless flood and people in our village are still talking about getting to America in some way or other.

*   *   *

JOSEPHINE, female domestic helper, 37

Hong Kong Special Administrative Region, southern China

'Let's just say 60 or 70 per cent of Filipinas felt abused by their employers in Hong Kong.'

ARRIVING IN HONG KONG was really exciting for me.

It was my first time abroad. I remember thinking that I could not get further away from rice farming anywhere on earth. I was so happy about making a better life . , . but, my Lord, the reality proved very different and Hong Kong was never a good experience.

My troubles started with Mr and Mrs Leung. They lived in a good part of town but in a very small apartment: one living room, one bedroom, and one tiny utility room off the kitchen for me. There was a miniature window and the toilet was very near my bed.

I created a good schedule of ironing and washing and cleaning. I did feel trapped inside the 500 square feet flat but there were shopping trips around the Mid-levels, which I enjoyed. And the salary was most definitely welcome. Paid regularly at the end of each month it was much more than I made in the Philippines.

Things changed.

After Mr Leung's promotion, which brought more travel and money, his wife resigned and spent her days at home. I tried disappearing to the kitchen while Ma'am relaxed in the living room or slept in the bedroom, but tension built. She began to raise her voice and after a while shouted demands for 'greater respect' and 'more loyalty'. Her rudeness made me angry and I started to wonder if I could last two years. . . .

Mr Leung provided an answer.

He had hired me via an employment agency. Coming home late one evening he said that he had asked them to change my contract. Just like that, oh my God, and I would have to live elsewhere. I could still work for them part-time, if I wanted, but must find alternative accommodation and give Mrs Leung peace at home. Or I could return to Luzon.

I argued it was not right changing contracts like that but learned that the law was on his side. I moved the following weekend.

Living out meant renting the bottom bunk in a windowless room. Eight people shared a single toilet and the kitchen was a converted cupboard. My bed smelled from insufficient air-conditioning. Everything was noisy from people coming and going, day and night, and you could hear screeching tram wheels often. Sleep was very difficult. Believe me, I will always remember that place.

Working several part-time jobs became very challenging. And it was illegal. Well, *subtly* illegal if you understand my meaning. Many maids did it, very many, but the police didn't enforce the law in those days. At one stage I had seven employers: one American family, some Koreans, three Chinese families and the Leungs.

Starting before dawn I would slip house-to-house until late evening. Pausing for a break where I could, eating lunch in a bathroom whilst pretending to clean behind the door. Anything for a rest. At six days a week, sometimes every day, it was exhausting.

The only positive news was more money for my parents who were looking after my son, and the local Church.

Two Chinese families asked me to become full-time and work for other friends of theirs and at their trading business doing clerical work. They fired me from part-time work when I refused.

'No good attitude,' they said to my face.

'Never again,' I silently thought. I knew they were going to work me like a slave and I could not escape for two years.

When the Americans left my monthly income dropped to HK$2,000. Most went on rent. But I still had hope.

Then came the abuse. . . .

Let me say even the smartest parts of Hong Kong have bad people that Jesus might find it hard to love. I have stories . . . shocking . . . I'm sorry. . . .

An employer started touching me.

He had an expensive apartment in Kowloon where he lived by himself. He hired me to clean cupboards and other work involving stretching upwards. He started casually touching my breasts. At first he pretended innocence, testing my reactions, but seeing little, I really needed that work, he continued into open rubbing.

I cried sometimes.

But his confidence had grown and my tears only created problems. Later came removal of clothes and demands to wash my body while he watched . . . it was horrible . . . I'm sorry again.

Not that I was alone.

Let's just say 60 or 70 per cent of Filipinas felt abused by employers in Hong Kong. Not necessarily physical or sexual mistreatment, like it was for me. But still a very real emotional exploitation, and that is just as bad.

Becoming legally estranged from my husband deepened the hate I was starting to feel for Hong Kong.

It was the city's fault. That's what I thought, somehow. Hong Kong had made him stop caring for me and for our son. Ernesto's disappearance from my life is still, in my heart, a legacy of Hong Kong.

The week my divorce filing arrived I resigned from the job with the pervert, who by then had initiated sexual relations. Which was ironic. I hated being disloyal to the holy institution of marriage. But as soon as it didn't matter, as soon as I was getting divorced, I ended the contact. I still can't explain that.

I thought work in Repulse Bay, a very high-class residential area, might deliver a fresh start. Richer people would surely be more decent? Wrong. They soon forced me to work on Sundays even though that was The Lord's Day of Rest, and they had previously said I would be free on that day to see my friends and attend church. Hours of garlic mincing for *kimchi* were mixed with cleaning and polishing their three cars, simply to see them dirty again within hours.

Disagreements appeared with their full-time maid. She was in her late forties and began shouting orders in rude Tagalog. She would contradict the boss's instructions too, just to cause trouble. I hadn't expected such conflict with one of my people.

Excuse my language but after four years I had realised Hong Kong was all about shit work. But returning home wasn't a realistic option. My parents needed more improvements to their house and my son still had years of school ahead of him, and hopefully college.

When Fernando reached middle school I found extra work as an assistant cook at a seafood restaurant. That was truly repulsive work and I was also given extra cleaning work after the restaurant closed.

Arguments started with a cleaner when I discovered she earned HK$8 per hour more. And for less work too. I couldn't complain to management because she was a permanent resident and I was still sort of illegal. But whenever we were alone sparks flew, my goodness, especially when she gossiped on the telephone with friends whilst I handled the hard work. I hated that.

Hearing *myself* swear in Tagalog worsened things. I never spoke like that in the Philippines. But she made me mad, especially when she claimed Hong Kong was Chinese now and I could leave anytime. That reminded me of Mrs Leung's cruel words.

Eventually her lies to a junior manager paid off and I was asked to leave. It was a relief, really.

Thankfully I quickly found work as a nanny for a Taiwanese family in the Mid-levels.

The kids enjoyed me. My kindness when they came across problems was better than the full-time maid who had become tired and unconcerned when they cried. But the whole experience reminded me of the home I was missing and the Taiwanese mother became rude for little reason. Perhaps she sensed a part of me hated caring for a Chinese child when in the back of my mind it was the Chinese that caused my separation from Ernesto. Crazy thinking, I know. But when she asked me to leave I was not disappointed very much.

Then came problems with my sister, the worst because they brought quarrels into my beloved family.

Employers from Tai Tam, another very select town in Hong Kong island, needed a replacement full-time maid. I was still against full-time work, but my sister Virginia didn't mind and was offered work provided she arrived promptly from the Philippines. All after a single telephone call. That was an encouraging sign, I thought, and they even paid Ginny's airline ticket and signed basic immigration papers in advance. Ginny arrived one afternoon and was at work by dinner.

Astonishingly the Chens changed their minds.

Coming to sign final employment papers — Ginny had been asked to live with me for the first month which I now realise was a trick — Ma'am simply refused to sign.

Ginny was totally stunned.

And I was in flashback: how could my experience with the Leungs be repeated? How could the Chens fly her hundreds of miles only to ditch her? And with not even basic human courtesy?

When I resigned in protest Mrs Chen retaliated by demanding Ginny pay for her air ticket. We shared some angry and very aggressive words. . . .

'That's completely unfair. You agreed to pay!'

'In that case we'll take it from your pay. She is your family.'

'That is *not* legal.'

'Complain to the police then. . . .'

Of course Mrs Chen knew about my visa problem so it was an abuse we had to take.

After Ginny joined me in my tiny bed space my stress level doubled. To save money we slept head-to-toe. Seeing her daily made me feel guilty at not predicting the Chens' deception. But I was also confused about what Ginny did wrong and why she refused to discuss the problem with me.

When Ginny became entangled in a separate court case, a very nasty battle that I supported financially as well as emotionally, the dishonesty of Hong Kong seemed to have reached even lower. For a while I thought breaking point had been reached and that we would both rather be poor in Luzon than poor and abused in Hong Kong.

A man wrote a probationary contract for Ginny ending on the 29th of the month, but secretly dated it '27' after she signed. He refused to let her keep a copy. Later he used the fake contract to trick Ginny into being an over-stayer so that he didn't have to pay her in full. Legally she had to be deported back to the Philippines. Thankfully, oh my Lord I'm thankful, we uncovered written proof of the deception from another maid who quietly photocopied another '29' contract. The employer was ordered to repay salary plus some compensation to Ginny.

But Hong Kong was too much by then and the instant of success Ginny returned home with her money; without much of a 'goodbye' either.

I couldn't blame her.

But we don't have much contact these days. Well, there is still tension between us, to tell the truth. I paid for Ginny's lawyers, you see, and every time that was HK$300 or sometimes HK$500, a large part of my salary. She never paid me back.

Despite the court case and Ginny's disappearance I stayed in Hong Kong.

By my late thirties I hope to have earned enough to open a restaurant in my home village. I still hope Ginny will join that though I don't think she'll like working for me; at least I won't deceive her contractually. I hope Fernando will help me when he graduates.

Hong Kong opened my eyes to very, very, tough conflicts and arguments and trickery. But I still really don't understand the hate and bad treatment . . . it's painful to discuss . . . it was so unnecessary.

Chinese employers, I should say, weren't the only abusers.

Please understand I'm not racist like many of *them*. I can tell you that maids employed by Koreans are unhappy too. European and American employers also cause unhappiness, though it's probably fair to say they are preferred employers. As to the Japanese, well, put it like this: a Japanese family once invited me to work for them in Japan but I refused. That's a country of prostitution and they treat Filipinas very badly, even worse than the Chinese.

There are simply no guarantees.

But the worst were the Hongkongers. All of them, starting with Mrs Leung, would follow me around the house, watching and checking like guard dogs. Foreigners were more trusting and let me feel human. But the Hongkongers? They made me feel like a thief. Ginny laughed at the irony of their love for Confucius: *If you employ a man, be not suspicious of him; if you're suspicious of a man, do not employ him.* She read that from a book someone had left in our boarding house. But that's a living lie, let me tell you, a complete lie. Many Chinese never trust people like us.

Thankfully I am close to finishing the seven-year moratorium. Then I can be divorced in a final, legal, way. That's what I want. To be single again. And when I run my restaurant life can be as simple as it was before all this fraud and anger came into my life. I will always hate the conflicts Hong Kong created for me. I hate them for what they did, how they tricked me . . . deceived my sister . . . raped me.

*   *   *

WAI-LUN, male clerk, 28

Sichuan Province, southwest China

'True to their word, a further eight protestors were arrested. Killing a chicken to scare a monkey was obviously a fashionable police tactic.'

I HAD WORKED in Mr Hung's factory for several years when the workers blocked the road.

'The only way to split open Mr Hung's dishonesty! Before it is too late!' The only reason the factory is being sold to Taiwanese people is criminal dishonesty! It has nothing to do with the workers' bad efforts!'

And as cars turned around loud cheers would build up, like waves crashing on a beach.

By then I knew enough to be unsurprised that the police arrived quickly, ready to dismantle the problem and silence the cheers as usual. Eight protestors were arrested that time and their alleged crimes shouted over loudhailers: 'Guilty of anti-city, anti-modernisation scheming,' the police had broadcast, or some such lie that Mr Hung liked to hear. The road was re-opened and the troubles downgraded once more to ghosts that only workers saw.

Later that night Mr Hung banqueted important police officers and some 'loyal workers', which meant accountants like me. A senior policewoman said the worker reactions seemed to go against both public safety laws and the will of the state. Treason might be charged if more road-blocking happened.

Yet another fast-talking Sichuanese businessman was getting his way.

Antics after dinner were especially embarrassing that night. Mr Hung tried repeatedly to give the senior policewoman *another* bottle of cognac in appreciation for her loyalty.

'But it's a sensitive time in the Party and I can't accept favours,' she argued, unconvincingly but loudly enough for all to hear.

Mr Hung smiled as if her words meant nothing and that there had never been a pool of wine and a forest of meat in front of them. 'But what of your husband?'

And finally, after some deep exchange of views about the bribery problem in Sichuan and the importance of setting a good example she conceded: 'Well, I suppose that would be acceptable. He is one of the workers.'

And for the first time I wanted to shout that the protestors were correct in attacking Mr Hung.

I knew the truth. His criminal money came from the padlocked sales boxes collected from shops around the city. Regularly piles of smelly notes would appear inside a tiny office with no windows and a small light. Mr Hung personally managed the in-and-out door.

He insisted I, and no other, sit at the solitary table and count the money. After reviewing my figures and sometimes after searching my pockets or shoes, even at times my underpants, he would quietly send me back to the main office before taking the bound cash to his office. A while after, sometimes an hour and sometimes a day, he would send another accountant to deposit it in the bank.

He always emphasised secrecy.

'It is a necessary secret that protects us from bad effects. You must never have discussions about deposit amounts.'

Based on informal words with other accountants, I estimate Mr Hung deceived workers for about 25 per cent, but that could be an underestimate. Certainly in absolute terms it was several millions of yuan over the years, enough to pay cash for his three houses and those cars and the rest of his impressive things.

Unfortunately for Mr Hung there was a prominent 'Go West, Support All Chinese' conference. You know the sort of thing: higher-ups pretend to create important plans for other higher-ups to hear, even though everyone knows even they can't create something from nothing.

Protesting workers saw the conference as a chance to reach friendly journalists in Chengdu.

They travelled *en masse* but regrettably the newspapers showed little interest. Accusations about Mr Hung's bribes sounded boring, so it seemed, and tearful confessions from a former worker sacked for trying to quantify Mr Hung's crooked takings also had no effect. The workers soon became frustrated.

Mr Hung had taken myself and a few others to monitor things and watched with pleasure as the protests died like flowers without water.

At dinner he entertained some city police officers and senior officials, playing point at the mulberry bush to criticise the locust and declaring there were many protestors he didn't recognise. 'It must be a problem of false pride in the workers. Nothing to do with me personally. They are very old, bored people looking for something to do.'

It was becoming harder to hide my anger about his deceit.

My feelings worsened when junior police officers dispersed what was left of the protestors the following day. True to their word a further eight protestors were arrested that afternoon. Killing a chicken to scare a monkey was obviously a fashionable police tactic.

Mr Hung ordered me to take RMB65,000 from his account in the *Bank of China.* I was to distribute the cash to three police officers in the proportion of 3:2:1, each sweetener hidden within cognac gift-sets. He was unbothered if it was genuine Hennessy; as long as it looked expensive.

That night I couldn't sleep.

Looking over the moonlit hibiscus trees of Chengdu I questioned my participation in such obvious dishonesty and it was a defining moment of my life.

I left a short note explaining my decision: I didn't know the city well and was inexperienced. Not wanting to fail him, if he wished to cooperate with the police it would be better he do so himself.

I doubted the disobedience would fool him, nor the lie that I must leave to resume work back home. Apart from counting money I did nothing much. I hoped to trick him into lowering his defences whilst gaining me time.

After several days I bought dinner for a policeman from another part of the city.

I explained how Mr Hung had regularly stolen money and named the three police officers in Chengdu taking Mr Hung's bribes. He was also cheating tax officials so he could get credit as part of the Strike Hard campaign, maybe even destroy other people like the vice-mayor. Anti-organised crime was a big issue in those days.

Unfortunately it became clear that strategy works both ways.

Hung quickly knew I was still in Chengdu and that I had spoken to other police officers. He shouted down the phone that if I thought I could sneak down the Cheng Chang passage I would pay the full price for my disloyalty. He even knew my hotel room and an ex-colleague arrived within an hour to demand my train ticket home. I would have to pay for my own trip back.

My policeman contact was deaf and blind. He reluctantly agreed to meet but only in a small and distant restaurant.

He arrived full of stories and apologies: unemployment was very high in our area so selling the factory as Mr Hung intended was, in his eyes, probably a good way to save people's jobs. Foreigners would bring more investment. 'Perhaps Mr Hung is reasonable,' he finished but it sounded like: *And you are a liar.*

When I asked which forces had warned him against taking an interfering interest he became angry: 'You should avoid connection with anti-authority forces. Don't make me part of your scheming.' And he walked off, leaving food uneaten and with me to pay the bill once more. I never saw him again.

Forced to leave Chengdu and return home, jobless and with a powerful enemy to face, I felt terrible and worried.

But sometimes the heavens have mercy.

Mr Hung never sent police or others to harm me as I feared. I guess he knew I would not find other work with such good pay, that

I would have to ride an ox for a long time before I could find another horse.

Looking back I regret most of all involving that policeman in Chengdu.

Simply because you have an honest story, or even evidence about real bank accounts, it doesn't necessarily benefit you. In fact there is *every* chance that honest efforts harm you if even one of the people in authority have relations with your enemy. Truth often finds the strongest enemies.

If the heavens gave me my choices once more I would have kept silent and showed loyalty as unquestioning as a hungry dog. And if I kept quiet I would still have a good job at Mr Hung's factory, instead of trivial work in shops. Perhaps even Mr Hung would have allowed me, one day, to take some bonus money for myself. Or I might have worked out a way to hide money inside my body. I know that sounds as bad as the police, or even Mr Hung himself, but when you end up like me whilst everyone else seem to be taking bribes and you wonder if honesty really pays.

Recently I heard that one of the policeman I was meant to bribe in Chengdu, I'm sure it was him from the list of names Mr Hung gave me, was arrested for taking bribes and having unaccountable possession of many American dollars. Apparently he also had a huge collection of cognac bottles.

*   *   *

YAN, male personal assistant, 47
Guangdong Province, southern China

'He wants to call the local partner a cheating turtle-egg yet his tone is deeply Confucian and reserved. . . .'

THE COMPANY WHERE I WORK lost so much money in Foshan.

From reading my boss's e-mails I can tell that from an agreed investment of US$18 million, signed about ten years ago, the Guangdong partner has now got over US$50 million. In return my boss pays over 90 per cent of the bills for 45 per cent ownership of what he once wrote was, and this is an exact quote, *an unprofitable mess which shows no real prospects and is embarrassing our brand.*

You can best understand things with these excerpts; don't read the whole letter; it's too long. But in the important parts you can see my boss wants to call the local partner a cheating turtle-egg. Yet his tone is very Confucian and reserved. I still don't know why.

Our company manages design-and-build projects of European-style housing communities. Our partner is a state-owned enterprise specialising in steel moulding. They claim they went into real estate to create prestige and better connections.

To my dear friend and business partner —

Because we stay far away in Hong Kong and cannot help with your daily fires and struggles we ask little and complain rarely. But you must know we feel 'heron-faced, pigeon-shaped' as we have no food for our efforts. Please allow me to explain our shared situation so we can maintain good communications and resolve our problems through the qualities of equality and self-willingness.

Our original terms of cooperation were US$18 million for fifteen years.

At your insistence this was enlarged to fully US$47 million for twenty years. You said local market conditions were 'close enough to burn your eyebrows' [facing serious competition]. No matter the amount or schedule, the change was caused by your demands. We signed as if we were under your city wall [being coerced] but honoured our shared desires for success. Now you tell my managers it might take over thirty years to create profit. How can you make me lose face in front of my staff? Can you see my true sadness at what you say to me with one face and to my staff with another face?

Now you require US$4.25 million (US$5,000 x 850 houses) for owner-ship transference fees before we can sell the houses. I find no previous mention of this fee. In truth, since we signed both the memorandum-of-understanding and the contract, many years ago, land and buildings are still owned by you. Your company did not observe the contract terms and transfer them to our joint venture. Why did this happen? Do you consider this an example of 'bad faith following good words'?

Leasing of the first 35 houses led to huge losses for our joint venture. Strangely these early tenants secured very cheap rent, not even half of similar properties nearby. Stories say that they are your connections or relations of your staff. Is this negligence? If your negligent employees stay unpunished and the tenants continue paying such little money, how can we continue with confidence?

The Phoenix Resident's Club is unprofitable whilst our other clubs in Taiwan and Korea make profits of up to 25 per cent even during their early years of operation. Your supervisor is not an expert in this business and you have a personal involvement with her, acting in your words as a 'grindstone to each other' [to create improvements]. But after several years I can see little advancement despite much expense and effort.

It puzzles me that you are indifferent to losses of US$230,000 through payment of compensation to some departing staff. Your location in the 'Little Empire' of the People's Affairs Department prevented my staff from cancelling payments or acting properly by good business standards.

As a state enterprise you must honour proclamations from the Central Government and provincial leaders in Guangdong. You should serve their 'Make Glory From Hardships' wishes but I only see you fight for money and personal advantages and create defeats for us as the minor partner, who has, by the way, given the majority of money.

There is an old belief that some situations make going forwards or backwards equally impracticable. We could arrive in this situation soon if we do not help ourselves. The best solution therefore is that you become sole owner and return our money with interest. Then you will have the houses and the Phoenix Clubhouse and can make the money you promised was possible.

Without this approach, you must understand that, with much regret, we have no other viable choices but to make the unfairness in the situation bright and obvious [seek justice]. This will be a disaster and we will both suffer a harmed reputation. Like tall Banyan trees attracting strong winds we will suffer. So please join me in ensuring this does not happen and that we are serious about mutually supporting each other.

I am always your friend and business partner. . . .

It's sad to read that again. It refreshes memories of the regret that followed early optimism and hope. There was a time when my boss was certain Guangdong Province offered a great future for our company and that we had finally found the right partner.

Will the money reappear?

Maybe. I hope so. He deserves some satisfaction because he is a good man.

But it is several months since this letter was sent. Nothing seems to have changed and my boss has not startled any snakes just by rustling the grass. The local partner is as rude and silent as usual. I don't even think they acknowledged receiving the letter, though perhaps they said something verbal that I don't know about.

I don't think anyone in our company believes the partner would submit to settlement based on a Hong Kong-style legal process. They know we would require very strong connections to force them to be fair and return the money.

In my eyes, and many other small-potato staff around our company, that US$50 million plus is as good as gone. Only the boss will not accept this view. Not publicly anyway. That is unrealistic.

The key mistake was continuing investment despite seeing little return. We would never do that in our lives or our marriages so why do rich people do it in business? It sounds crazy. And with so much money too. Postponing conflict in circumstances like this is the worst strategy. Once he agreed to pay a further US$29 million it was predictable that he would be asked for a further US$4.25 million. Then other money. It was obvious that he would suffer more abuse and tricks.

And now it is too late for him; it's just too late. . . .

*   *   *

CHI-LING, female assistant worker, 49

Anhui Province, eastern China

'My loose mouth had been noted after all, and would be used to cause problems for me.'

MY GREAT MISTAKE was opening my mouth in social settings.

I had worked for ten thousand days in that office so I should have known much better.

Workers often used idle words to create problems for others if they could find a personal advantage. But something got the better of me that night. Perhaps it was finally winning some money at the *mahjong* table.

And before I knew the wind had blown my mouth spouted about my foolish outlook. The boss's wife had very poor knowledge about production targets, I said, and I remember even laughing. How stupid of me to laugh. Her advice should be ignored for everyone's benefit, I even added.

How stupid I was that night. Not even four horses could catch those words.

Immediately there was a problem. After a hush some uncomfortable laughs broke the silence but for weeks afterwards people gave me odd looks. I regretted it greatly and hoped people would either forget my words or treat them as a foolish accident.

But I was not so lucky.

During the Dragon Boat festival, the boss's wife requested my company because her husband was in Beijing and I was officially the secretary of the production department.

During the meal afterwards she was very cold and distant.

As I travelled to her home and in full view of the driver she aired her negative feelings out loud: *'What makes you think I can't offer advice about production?'*

'Please believe me,' I tried to say as the car dropped her off, 'Whatever you heard I never said your opinion had no worth or tried to slander you. It was just a casual and meaningless comment that people have misunderstood. Stupid talk.'

'No use denying it!' she shouted back. 'You spat blood on me! You are a disloyal and lying element! I have to wonder what else you have said about me?'

It was a few days before I could speak privately with my boss.

'Why did you two fight?' he asked, sipping his tea as he read some faxes from overseas.

And so I had explained, as cautiously and apologetically as possible, that I never planned to start any argument or splittist manoeuvrings. It was just accidental words. Or his wife had been misinformed about a few of my words.

'No contributions.' My boss raised his eyebrows, suddenly interested. 'Did you really say that?'

I said once more that it was nothing more than women's talk around the *mahjong* table that had grown out of proportion due to miscommunications and errors in sharing understanding.

'I understand,' he nodded. 'But I will have to talk with my wife and evaluate her version of events.'

I was worried sick.

Later that week he called me to his office, still very thoughtful and cautious in his words. It was quite difficult to guess his thoughts. 'There is a difficult problem. I cannot solve it myself. To help calm her fires you will need to write a self-criticism letter.'

'What should I say?'

'Say you made a mistake.'

'Only that?'

'Tell her that you did not intend anything bad.'

'All that is true,' I agreed.

'But after your apology you can add a "but". You can deny her attacks, as you did when we talked; emphasise that you never meant to sow discord.'

'That's also true,' I agreed again, seeing for the first time some chance of solving the problem.

The boss showed his wife the letter and said it passed inspection. However, I would have to do more to completely solve the problem. 'Start talking a little nonsense with the other staff. Mention some false numbers. Confuse dates. Say Europe when you mean Australia. And make sure my wife gets to hear about your foolish words.'

That was hard but I had no choice. It was deliberate mistakes to give his wife more face or lose my job. No alternative.

It worked though. A few weeks later the boss and I were discussing a business plan and he quietly said: 'About the problem with my wife. Not to worry. It is over. Your efforts have been successful.'

So for me it was a lucky escape. Let me tell you that those foolish words could have easily cost me my job. It confirmed that there are some good bosses in Anhui who know how to resolve conflict very well, you know. Even if they ask you to criticise yourself or make yourself look stupid they still know how to achieve something positive.

the young

Most Chinese today were born after Deng Xiao-ping initiated his economic reforms. They know and remember not pure Chinese communism, if there is or was such a thing, but instead the blossoming of a hundred cultures, all rushing to capitalism, rather than the time when a single communist culture and way of thinking was deemed fit for one and all.

HONG-GUO, female AIDS victim, 16

Heilongjiang Province, northeast China

'Mr Soong knew there were people with AIDS in the area and he wanted them gone, no matter the method.'

SHADE HAD DOMINATED our family's fields like Chairman Mao once did the country.

It all happened after Mr Soong illegally permitted the construction of the Party offices. He only considered his bribe, of course. Like the other officials money was the only thing. Like a deaf thief stealing a bell he ignored our warnings of the bad effects that eighteen-storey buildings can have on farmland.

Trust me, he said. The offices and shops will benefit everybody for generations. He told that lie to parents and their compatriots for months and months and months.

After a few harvest seasons it became clear that we were right all along. The lack of sun caused by the high buildings *did* cause less and less successful harvests compared to the other side of the valley.

The worst result for our family was that as our harvest reduced Papa could only give smaller and smaller red packets to Mr Soong and the other officials at Lunar New Year. The village couldn't pay for banquets and other entertainment with the Party officials. That was a slow death sentence. Mr Soong became more and more unhappy. We started to get less favourable treatment at tax collecting time, worsening our money problems and harming our relations with the authorities.

Then came the floods.

'I have to explode one dam!' Mr Soong had shouted at Papa as the rains battered down. Then he hastily ordered the emergency army troops to demolish the north dam. First explosions failed because they weren't real engineers although they said the central authorities had trained them. That must have been a lie. But eventually a massive eruption released tonnes of muddy water through our fields. It ruined the crops, naturally it would, which were swept away in a moment. The soil remaining was badly harmed and reminded me of brown glue; it was useless for growing.

The water also toppled many farm buildings.

I don't think Mr Soong expected concrete pilings to give way that easily. But they hadn't been improved for many years because of the money problems he caused.

Mr Soong may have been surprised at the collapsed homes but he wasn't upset at such dramatic outcomes. Mr Soong, you see, well, he knew there were people with AIDS in the area and he wanted them gone, no matter the method.

AIDS had all happened like this.

Seeing the results of his decisions, he had attempted to keep people quiet by sending mobile blood-collecting hospitals to our village. Naturally he guessed people would be desperate for money from the hospitals. The hope was he would get better face for himself by helping 'his people' with some extra money, and we would shut up with complaints about his illegal buildings and other dishonesty.

Hospital staff had collected blood over the years but they never used new needles for each person. It was unfair to pay for them as well as Mr Soong's arrangement fee, their doctors claimed, and so they cleaned the needles with tissues and hot tap water. They said tests in Beijing showed this was good enough.

Sadly we've learnt that AIDS isn't so easily prevented.

And we've also discovered that as people became sicker and sicker, especially when we always seem to have river-fish sickness, diarrhoea, then other people start to avoid you.

Once the true tests finally confirmed the situation, instead of helping our people, like Party leaders should, Mr Soong's reaction was to get his cronies to cover up the whole affair. None of the authorities in his circle came with real help. Instead they looked to the east or the west, turning a blind eye to our problems and a deaf ear to our words.

He was very unhappy when anti-AIDS drugs started to arrive from another provincial authority where he had no connections.

Our people were so sick by then, Papa had no choice but to stop working, so Mr Soong couldn't really complain loudly. But he quietly made sure we only got the cheap domestic medicines, the ones that made people sick, and sure enough the inhabitants of our village stopped taking them after a while.

'How can I be blamed for that?' Mr Soong would demand of anyone challenging him, and walk away as if nobody understood the real situation, as if we were all trying to act as guides for the tiger and find a scapegoat.

Eventually Papa and some others created a petition for Mr Soong. They demanded that he use Party funds to pay for the right medicines.

Mr Soong refused: 'Nationally-made medicines are always good enough,' he wrote in a public reply.

But I'm sure in his heart hew knew that most of us would rather be sick than take those medicines. I can never take them and I am the strongest of our family. Papa's breathing becomes almost impossible with them.

So most of our people are dying, and all of us are becoming poorer each year too.

Meanwhile Mr Soong sits in his big office, drinking his cognac, watching his satellite television and is unpunished for his crimes. Sometimes I see him through his window, overlooking our dark and ruined land, and infected people trying to grow something. It is as if we have nothing to do with him and are merely characters in one of his television dramas. 'Sacrifice the little things to achieve the big plan,' I once heard him say to Papa.

*   *   *

PHOENIX, male designer, 23

Shenyang, Liaoning Province, northeast China

'For ages Mr Tang had tried to hide the numbers, so I broke into his computer one night. . . .'

BY MY MID-TWENTIES I could no longer avoid returning to Shengyang.

I had put it off for as long as I dared. I loved California and I would have stayed in LA if, like, there was any choice, you know. But my Dad needed help expanding the production side of the business in Shenyang.

And as he and Mom had paid my college tuition, I guess, for so many years it only seemed right to work as a manager, for a while. Even though Dad knew living there for me, especially with its dirt and all that cruelty to animals thing, was, like, way down on my list of ambitions. I still don't really understand why he was always super enthusiastic about the country.

After a while I felt something was like way wrong with a deputy manager called Mr Tang.

Dad employed him to run things when he was out of town. He e-mailed me that he was confident in his honesty. He was certain that he would not steal our leather-engraving technology and stretching techniques. At any rate, Dad thought, our patterns and styles were updated so often to keep up with trends in the States it would be difficult for anyone to set up an operation to compete with us.

I wasn't convinced.

And as I was at the sharp end, actually living there, I started to explore around the city, bored out of my mind from nothing to do at work.

Dad was out of touch. There were, like, a hell of a lot of counterfeit products on sale that used our special techniques. I found street markets in the far west of the city where several of our unique designs from that month were displayed, sometimes showing our customer's brands. Which like was so weird, you know. The first time that happens it freaks you out and you go: *What the fuck is with that?*

There was no way simple pilfering could explain so many of our products for sale. I was way sure of that.

So naturally I had asked Mr Tang, pretty casual and all, why this might be happening. At first he replied that he didn't know. Right. That alerted me, you know, to a major problem straight off the bat because he usually had an opinion about anything to do with the factory. Often he disagreed with me if he could so this was the first time he had nothing to say for himself.

When I pushed some more he wondered if it might be other factories sending people to see what was happening in the American market. And bullshit like that alerted me even more.

By then I was on a mission to really get this guy. His whole story was just so unlikely because our designs changed every few weeks.

Seeing he had not convinced me, he started to come up with stuff about the provincial fight against fake goods. 'Liaoning certainly has shortcomings,' he smiled at me as if he was The Wise Old Man of the province. 'The people should try to correct this bad image through greater efforts. They should become more self-disciplined.'

Freaky, very freaky.

I started to look at the turnover of our staff because for ages Mr Tang tried to hide the numbers from me. I broke into his computer one night. Not really ethical admittedly but by then I had my suspicions.

And what do you know?

I discovered probably half of our staff had worked for a few months in our factory, maybe a little more, before being hired by another company, one with a very similar name to ours. And *that* was information that Mr Tang should not have had. That was my smoking gun right there.

I snooped around some more, that was kind of fun actually, going into someone's PC. It was like being a private eye.

As well as having many files about that other company Mr Tang had also saved design drawings for our machines. There were also soft copies of technical manuals that he definitely should not have had.

Already it was more than enough for me to act.

But knowing Dad and his loyalty to Mr Tang, to triple-check I visited the other factory the next weekend, all innocent like.

And I was amazed how familiar it looked. Even their logo was similar, the colour scheme too, and their price catalogue was uniformly cheaper than ours. No matter what the product everything was about ten per cent less. It was freaking eerie.

Enquiries by one of my contacts revealed that a crony of Mr Tang owned the competitor factory. That guy had sometimes appeared around our factory and I had kind of said hello occasionally. So that was another thing, finding people you had been buddying-up with who had been polite to your face were stabbing you in the back.

Dad arrived a week later.

I guess he was pretty shocked at the news. He sacked Mr Tang straight up, though not before taking his computer away to check for himself. That opened his eyes, believe me.

Within a few weeks Tang had given up all pretences and appeared at the rival factory as the joint manager.

And we have been pretty much rivals since then.

In fact, well, these days it's practically impossible to find honest staff who won't take our latest design to Tang and his buddies. It is so bad that Dad is starting to think about leaving Shenyang altogether and setting up in Mexico, which might be cool. There would be a lot less travel time for sure and the beer is better there.

I guess Dad hoped to shut the door and catch the thief. But that proved impossible and Tang has never faced any police investigation, despite our requests and relationship building with key figures in authority. All that talk of the WTO protecting intellectual property and brands and stuff like that? It's a joke, man.

And it shows you: if you really want to make it there, you need to keep an eye on the local situation. No matter if your products are being 100 per cent exported, or you think your staff are honest, there is a definite, like total, possibility that someone is building a copy-cat operation or may be taking bribes to reveal secrets. As well as walking around the local markets to see what is on sale, one of the most important things I would say is to get into the workers' computers on a regular basis.

The saddest thing is that Tang killed a little of Dad's love for the country. Even though our investment has been all but wasted, and that is never good, this loss of love is the real kicker for me. I sometimes wish it wasn't me that had to reveal everything to my Dad. . . .

*   *   *

WU, male salesman, 24

Chongqing Municipality, near Sichuan in southwest China

'They brought me some special soup, it was very good tasting, but within a few minutes I fell into a sort of paralysis.'

I HAD BEEN VISITING those people for six months when it happened.

Our business relations had been harmonious. In fact they were very good to me. So good that I started to bring more samples with me at the same time as I delivered the ordered watches.

After a while they started to say that even more samples and what they called 'pre-orders' was only fair. I should have been suspicious but some orders were worth tens of thousands of yuan, sometimes more. It was a lot of money so I tried to keep them happy, shutting my eyes to any scheming they might have in mind.

In return they paid for a young girl to show me interesting places around the city like parks and restaurants and museums. She looked after me at night as well.

On the night of the attack I had been away for a month. I returned to Chongqing with my largest batch of watches, easily worth RMB300,000, and I also had other merchandise with me that they considered a pre-order.

To celebrate they brought some special soup in the hotel room. Behind closed doors was where we always did our business to avoid spying eyes. And it was very good tasting winter melon soup, full with chunks of smoked ham.

They had none. 'Not hungry,' they said. . . .

Within a few minutes I fell into a sort of paralysis. It was quite amazing. I could see and hear nearly as normal, which was weird and frightening at the same time, like I was trapped in ice. I was aware that they were hurriedly moving around the room taking the watches and my telephone. They took my wallet too.

From the side of my eyes I saw them pocket my membership cards and railway tickets but I was unable to move my head or speak.

After they emptied my luggage I heard them go into the bathroom and take my jade bracelet and other private things. They took the other watches from the room safe. I still don't know how they knew the code number, but the hotel staff were certainly quiet afterwards.

Before leaving they put a DO NOT DISTURB sign on my door, loosened my tie and poured some water over my forehead. It must have helped to cool the drug's effects because in a few minutes I felt tingling in my feet and hands . . . movement gradually returned.

After the paralysis finally wore off I crawled to bed then fell into a massive sleep. It wasn't until the following afternoon that I came back to life.

Naturally I telephoned to demand the watches and my money.

But their business card proved false and their telephone number had been cancelled. Their office turned out to be a shopping centre with a thousand dealers and sellers so there was no way to find them there.

The hotel security manager said I had imagined everything. It sounded like I was seeing howling wind and screaming cranes because of strong wine. I certainly should not bother reporting crazy robberies like this to the police, he said.

I knew it was pointless to make an official complaint. The police would just side with the hotel and receive free meals and accommodation later.

And I definitely did not want any problems with the police over counterfeit property. As the security manager warned, out-of-town people like me were frequently punished more easily and had to pay large fines.

So I left it.

Amazing, isn't it? You can do business with people over months. Establish relations. And yet they are planning to rob you from the start, to lure a tiger from his mountain. And with drugs too. . . .

*   *   *

WAI-LEUNG, male interior designer, 26

Taipei, Taiwan

'Throughout the depositions and legal drama that followed, however, more and more I felt that the whole thing was an over-reaction by my brother.'

LIFE LOOKED EXCITING and uncomplicated when Peter employed my brother and myself.

I had just graduated from art school so getting a job with a foreign interior designer who we had studied was very welcome.

Peter was a long-term resident. Although Taiwan-style in some ways he still appeared to me as an Australian in his approach to design and to life. He was fairly famous in Taipei's arts scene and had a very fashionable client list. Someone who had successfully mixed East and West, the magazines said.

His company was called Design Minds.

Basically he decorated rich people's apartments, usually based around new tiling or paint schemes. Some designs were as ugly as hell, to my eyes anyway, but attractive and creative work was also produced, particularly when Peter was able to introduce European art furniture. Design Minds had started small, just Peter and one assistant, but there were six staff when we arrived and enough paperwork to need my elder brother's accounting expertise.

My job was to manage the painting process and order furniture or special lighting. It was often boring but I didn't mind. I was really, really, pleased to find such a job.

It became clear that Peter's business was financially quite weak.

At times, in fact, we could not move for lack of money. Staff sometimes waited several weeks for salary until an order was paid. When there was money, yes, at those times I would say Peter was pretty fair. But during the times of no money, well, the morale was quite low.

Morale fell even more when Peter started a second business in specialist paint manufacture. This involved quite a lot of his time and energy, and some of mine too as his assistant. Yet he never gave anybody shares or more pay. My brother started to complain about unpaid overtime required to handle the paperwork for Peter's second firm.

Despite everything, though, Peter built quite a good relationship with me.

Completing our first apartment felt great. It was a very big house west of Taipei and after we received the final cheque Peter took me for a celebratory drink. We became so drunk that his stories of being fired from two previous jobs was about the only thing I remembered from that night.

My brother, on the other hand, disliked Peter more and more. They often had communication problems. On that drunken night, for example, he made excuses to miss the celebration and refused to give Peter face for completing such a big job. Through his eyes Peter was friendless and arrogant: 'Like an academic. Thinks himself intellectually invincible.'

I didn't like that tension but said nothing for quite a long time, perhaps all of my first year at Design Minds. I didn't want to make it worse, I just wanted cooperation. . . .

Perhaps due to the new paint company, perhaps market conditions, business dried up next autumn and Peter only paid himself at Christmas.

My brother's anger boiled when Peter took his family on holiday.

'It must end cooperative relations!' he demanded of everyone, though I would hardly say he tried to keep them harmonious before. 'It is simply *wrong* for the foreign boss to take his family to Kenting for Christmas and leave the Taiwanese with no salary. . . .'

I disliked all the foreign-versus-local talk but never found a chance to disagree because plans directed by my brother had quickly, very quickly, emerged for a competing operation.

Predicting liabilities with the carpenters and decorators and other workers, my brother ruled against a sort of *coup d'état.* Peter should pay all bills. Instead, and still I don't quite know why I agreed to this, I was quite passive as everything happened, we tendered our resignations in a single letter. This was signed by everyone and placed on Peter's desk.

Adding a very cruel gesture my brother contacted a famous design magazine: Peter had stolen their ideas and evidence existed at such-and-such an apartment I heard him say on the telephone. I don't know what happened but I bet it caused problems.

It certainly was not the Happy New Year Peter might have expected after his holidays.

My brother's case for unpaid salary and bonus, which he posted with a government agency in Taipei, mostly failed. Several agreements with Peter turned out to be verbal, especially about bonuses, and I quickly learnt that words are tough to link with dollars, particularly when your opponent is uncooperative. Peter was understandably angry and probably felt very betrayed. He initiated legal actions against us for 'taking advantage of his demise', or some such legal phrase. Basically we were accused of fishing in troubled waters.

In return my brother sought legal aid to fight back. Properly this time, he promised.

Even though things still centred on unpaid salary and bonus there was now an emotional desire in my brother to, well, as he often said, fuck Peter up in court. It had become like that.

As the conflict heated up my brother demanded that we be more united. He wanted me to repeat under oath Peter's 'confession' that he had been fired twice for incompetence. That would humiliate him.

Through the legal drama, however, I started to feel the whole thing was an over-reaction. There was certainly no need to humiliate each other. The Buddhists have a good way of looking at this: 'Hate never ceases by hatred, only by love.' And when the court ruled there was no case I was not as disappointed as my brother.

Perhaps as a reflection of his failure to fuck Peter over in court my brother found some other troubles in our new company instead.

He focused on Ding, a designer who had also been in Design Minds and the catalyst was our staff.

My brother wanted to fire the head salesman, who he thought was not working enough for his salary. But the good friendship between the salesman and Ding prevented him.

After promises of improved efforts nobody was fired, that time, but to maintain smooth operations three teams emerged: design for the new houses, run by Ding; production and decoration-management, myself; and sales, run by my brother. Each of us was to cooperate generally but it became clear that my brother wanted it to be MYOB: Mind Your Own Business.

Creating little empires, however, didn't end tensions.

When my brother pushed first the head salesman, then another, to resign nobody spoke up. But I could feel Ding's resentment; in his eyes it was unnecessary harshness. In return my brother grew increasingly antagonistic towards Ding's laid back approach to expenses and preference for expensive materials.

Eventually Ding started to fight back.

Sometimes after their fighting words one of them had to leave for a few hours. I remember thinking after one huge argument that despite the money problems with Peter we never had tensions that bad.

Our relationship worsened. My brother began to privately hammer for me to side against Ding. He wasn't accusing me of disloyalty outright. But he suggested I might be conditioned and influenced subconsciously by Ding, and Peter before that. When he said I was an 'automatic dog robot' to my face I walked away and we didn't speak properly, brother to brother, for long periods. There was a steady tension and I really hated it.

I also hated how our business had become so, well, *functional* if you know what I mean. My brother was constantly asking: What do we gain from this? What is in that job for us? How much profit?

It was not why I had become a designer.

To cut a long and quite painful story short, those disagreements between myself and my brother, then between my brother and Ding, became so intense that my brother left. Now he has set up his own business providing accountancy services for small companies in Kaohsiung, where our family came from.

On the personal level I felt relieved.

But at a commercial level it left Ding and me facing a struggle. As business worsened we decided to reform an alliance with Peter, with whom we had always maintained basic contact without my brother's knowledge. He was much more approachable now that my brother had left.

Working with Peter again harmed my brother's attitude towards me but it proved a positive business move.

After a couple of years we started to go regional.

Peter secured two jobs in Shanghai after a trip, and each one, amazingly, included *business-class* flights and accommodation for Ding, Peter and myself. That was exciting. It made me realise splitting from Peter had been the wrong decision and I had been too influenced by my brother. Several years on now and we are active not only in Shanghai and Taipei but also in Los Angeles. And it looks like more work will come soon in Beijing.

My brother has cooled down a bit and we're back on basic speaking terms. I'm thankful for that I suppose.

He did show me that others emotionally influence me. And hassles do reduce my creativity and makes me depressed. I would never burn charcoal or anything drastic like that. But my psyche takes conflict harder than most. That I know from my brother.

I was brought up thinking collaboration with family members should be your first choice but I'm not sure anymore. Brothers or sisters with different views and ways of dealing with people won't always be effective together.

I suppose the biggest problem between us was his genuine belief that we had to share the same intolerances. When instead we disagreed, he became mad.

I think a lot came from our different approaches to Canada. My brother might have spent longer in Canada but he absorbed much less. From the start I had a real affinity and I felt great happiness for six years and never, ever, missed Taiwan. Were it not for the money I would jump on Air Canada for Toronto tomorrow. Most of my brother's friends in Canada were Chinese and he rarely spoke English.

Me . . . I guess I just integrated more and hung out in bars and places that my brother would look at and sneer.

*   *   *

PENG, female smuggler, 21

Liaoning Province, northeast China

'Another sixty thousand American dollars was the cost of my freedom, twice the sum that I had been caught smuggling. . . .'

I HAD BEEN DOING that particular cross-border run for several months when they finally arrested me.

They were always mistrustful of frequent trips to Vladivostok using tourist visas.

That's what the immigration officer had told me. But I looked into his eyes and could tell he was making a story from nothing. He saw my suspicious looks and added that unmarried women with no jobs to pay for holidays made them doubly suspicious. I knew he was lying. Someone had betrayed me.

Of course the bundle of American dollars made all of their eyes bulge like pregnant fish. If it was a pile of yuan they would have lost their breath, never mind something worth eight times as much.

That was when the big problems started.

They quickly pushed me away from the checkpoint into an old car with dark windows and curtains, put a hood over my head and hit me on my back and my legs.

At first I tried the cover story. I told them over and over that I was just carrying sealed packages and that I had no idea what they contained. Somebody in Harbin, an old man who I didn't know, had paid me and they would have to find out from him what the truth was. They sent some cronies off for a week but they came back with news that it was a fake address. Their beatings resumed. They demanded I tell my fellow criminals to send them American dollars before I was released.

They said they had already collected thirty thousand dollars from my luggage, which meant somebody was lying because there was fifty thousand when they trapped me. According to their common practices twice the sum that I had been caught smuggling, another sixty thousand American dollars, was the cost of my freedom.

And they were very determined.

They kept me for five months in that small house. Every few weeks, seeing nothing happen, they would put the phone in front of me and carefully monitor what numbers I called.

When they came to cause me sexual problems I feared for my life even more.

Tied up in a small room with only a little daylight, a mattress and a leaking tap, I felt very bad. It was constantly cold, especially at night, and the men kept laughing at me from behind the door when they had finished.

Thankfully they began to see that I was just nobody and no more money than the fifty thousand they had taken would come.

They finally released me.

They just dropped me at the train station with RMB500 and a knife at my throat while warning me not to speak out. After they pushed me out of their car it sped off with its siren blaring, as if they had to go and arrest the next criminal. Everything those criminals did was super-official.

My capture, I could hardly call it my arrest, was never mentioned in the papers. So those cheating officials must have kept the money for themselves.

And I never saw my boss again either. He must have fled when he learnt of my fate.

I just feel lucky to be alive, honestly. I am sure shady officers like that could have killed me for much less money. Being a small potato saved my life I suppose. But that can't happen twice in one life so I have to be careful now when I smuggle.

the old

China's elderly have a mindset wrapped in both the early optimism of revolution and the later pessimism of daily life under a regime that produced some great achievements but also failed to deliver on many of its pledges. Now that a certain wealth and comfort is finding some, there's a surfacing feeling that sacrifices have been ignored.

ZHAO-MING, male factory manager, 63

Shandong Province, eastern China

'He carefully waited until he could use a national ruling to his benefit and keep his key powers. . . .'

I'M STILL CONFUSED by the events, I don't have that clear feeling. . . . It wasn't the success I deserved after all those years. This is why people feel sorry for my situation.

Everything was arranged for me to take over the leadership role in my final years of work.

It certainly seemed natural and logical. I had worked for thirty-five years at the same factory; it is about 20 miles from here towards the Mount Taishan area. I joined in my twenties. It would have been just after I graduated from university if the Red Guards had not sent us to the countryside.

My job was always stable. I never changed loyalties unlike others who became greedy after the economic reforms. They changed companies often, sometimes for just a few yuan more.

Things went well because of my loyalty. I was promoted often and eventually became addressed as 'Deputy Manager Zhou'.

People truly believed I would soon control the factory. Many tried to build relationships with me in advance. They really did feel that I was the future, I am sure they did, and I received a lot of extra money and gifts in those days.

My clearest memory is Mr Keung telling people that my generation would succeed in modernisation and creating more profits. At a banquet with important local authorities he once again said he was happy about my succession: 'I have worked with Deputy Manager

Zhou for many years,' he announced to everybody. 'His character is good and loyal. There is a virtuous relationship.'

No date was given for the handover of power. But, as I say, his words were very clear; as clear as beautiful water you could say.

The end of the five-year plan in the late nineties would have been the most natural time for me to succeed. We looked likely to lose even more of our state-owned-enterprise status and would have to compete with other companies. Even though Mr Keung and I had quietly made informal arrangements to keep government contracts, this still meant earnest efforts. A new leader would be important.

Mr Keung, however, had other plans.

He jumped on a national ruling about retirement for his benefit.

First, he manoeuvred with cronies in the authorities. They made him head of the factory's Pensioners' Rights Committee and the Local Business Cooperation Committee. Both were powerful roles. Meanwhile a new role of 'Acting Manager' was made at the factory. This had less power than Mr Keung's old role and anyway he got one of his loyal cronies to fill it.

Second, he moved to better follow the national laws 'and other modernisation practices'. Which basically meant male workers aged over sixty had to leave immediately; 'no matter the seniority'. Of course he created a special rule so that he could stay himself: due to being leader of the Pensioners' Rights Committee he said. 'But that was the only exception.'

Older workers were shocked because national laws on retirement were often ignored in our area. Few had proper pensions, anyway, and simply worked until they were physically unable.

Some tried to seek justice from the authorities.

Mr Keung, however, had prepared for their attack and arranged for a high connection in the provincial Economic and Trade Commission to support his moves. We would all have to leave just as Mr Keung said.

I was singled out for special attention. Mr Keung angrily said that I could not 'seek to play tricks' by building connections with other authorities. The decision was final by national laws! 'Patriotic duty,' he said.

I tried private persuasion: 'If we cannot cooperate meaningfully this will affect the traditional strength of the factory.'

But this was brushed aside.

'We are independent now. The rules are different,' he concluded. Like he was forced into respecting the higher-ups with a heavy heart . . . the liar.

It's been a year now and Mr Keung is still in charge. Nobody challenges him.

That acting manager he brought in from the outside will soon be sixty. Only slightly younger than I was before Mr Keung killed my role. He has no real power. He just says what Mr Keung wants to hear. Mr Keung, on the other hand, he must easily be in his late sixties, some people say he's even older, but he never reveals his personal documents so who knows?

That's it, I suppose.

As I say, I still don't understand why Mr Keung tricked me from my rightful destiny. There is a saying we have in Shandong to describe this kind of behaviour: 'When the rabbits are dead, the dogs are boiled for food.' Past services and loyalty are soon forgotten.

Perhaps it was bad fate. Heaven or Mr Keung or somebody else up there never actually intended to give me the job.

Perhaps, though, there is another explanation that I've sometimes thought about lately — that actually I was too strong, like a big tail that the dog could no longer wag. Mr Keung could not attack me directly, you see, so he created a plan like attacking Wei to save Zhou.

Keeping me as heir apparent stopped people bothering to question his authority because they knew, they thought they knew, that one day he would be replaced. And so I relaxed when I should have been making preparations for battle and focusing on building relations with the provincial authorities and with important workers.

To this day, my dealings with the Economic and Trade Commission and other authorities have not become sharp knives. They only keep me happy with casual politeness.

And these days, few in the factory seem disturbed at the injustice handed to me. I should offer written documents, some have said, as if there were any. Others deny that they ever knew the details, which is a lie but, they know it can't be disproved.

I admit once trying to create strong passions in the workers' hearts and raise challenges against Mr Keung. But this started to make the workers irrational and dangerous judgements were becoming common. They could see Mr Keung still in control and started to ask: 'What's the good of supporting your position?' So they calmed down and I stopped trying to get justice that way.

It's wrong for people to make promises for years and years and then go back on their words. Some people can say anything today but, come tomorrow, they forget everything. People should *never* make my mistake of believing what people say to your face. Misdeeds can still happen no matter how many sweet words have been said, and older people can easily be the target of fraud and lies and trickery just as easily as young people.

*   *   *

MING-HUA, female manager, 61

Guangdong Province, southern China

'Never believe senior people invite genuine criticism. They will revenge themselves if your criticism puts them in even a little bad light.'

PAPA'S CONFLICT seemed endless at times.

He would continuously report back to Mama about his work supervisors and how bad they made life in the Dongguan Housing Bureau. Mostly I remember his passion, which was always critical and negative. At the bad times I almost felt he was begging into the hot and humid nights you get in the summer round here. Repeating things over and over. As if Mama could solve his problems.

Sometimes Mama would use her Buddhist ideals and try to relax him with kind words: 'I should prepare something, some nice food for you, you've worked so hard for me and the family.' But as she cooked Papa would just renew his talk of injustice, dishonesty, unfairness. . . .

Public holidays were the only real times Papa shared with my brother or me. Often after dinner he would spell out his beliefs about discretion in working life. 'No matter where or for whom you work,' he would stress, 'never believe senior people invite genuine criticism. They will revenge themselves if your criticism puts them in even a little bad light.' Sometimes there were tears in his eyes so we knew it was all about him.

One time my brother asked Papa if we should speak if we could see better methods. But that only distressed father and threatened to bring back his tears. Before walking off he replied angrily 'Even if you can see improvements, be quiet!' We never initiated the subject again.

Honest criticisms caused untold conflicts, that was the message.

As we grew up, though we always knew Papa had experienced problems, and that they were a great humiliation, we never really heard the details. My brother had a more adventurous side than me and sometimes he would say that Papa suffered for speaking stupid words during some Red Book campaign, or something else very political. But he never said it to his face.

Mama must have known the story but was content with silence. My brother didn't like that, and as we grew into the ways of Guangdong Province and the illusion that the revolution would create a favourable destiny for the people and for our family, he laughed more and more at Papa and his secret complaints. 'If Papa's past criticisms were valid,' he once claimed in front of Mama, 'the officials would have treated him fairly; they wouldn't let a good person go abused.'

By then, I suppose, I also thought that the mistake was Papa's, a little anyway, that genuine gold fears no fire, but I never said anything so directly as my brother.

As the years passed, and perhaps in response to our uncaring attitude, Papa began to show his angry face more at home.

Sometimes he shouted loudly within our farmhouse about the senior figures at his workplace. 'Guilty of all sorts of deceptions and high crimes!' Later he took to yelling about provincial leaders in Guangzhou, and even people in Beijing like Chairman Mao, for whom Papa had a very great hate. When Mama made him keep his voice down he would whisper that the Chairman 'lied east, lied west' when he claimed that the Party feared no criticism because Marx said truth was on their side. The Gang of Four should have been the Gang of Five if Mao hadn't died. But he never repeated that too loudly. It was a dangerous time to say such things and Mama thankfully made him keep quiet for the good of the family.

Finally losing his job blackened Papa's mood permanently. I don't think I saw him truly happy again.

He looked for work around Dongguan but nothing emerged. Other government offices seemed keen to avoid him and his connections sounded well meaning, or so Mama said, but proved unhelpful.

Our tiny farm on the southern side of Dongguan, it was only a handful of *mu* able to carry a few pigs and chickens and vegetables, had to provide for eight people as other family members lived with us. Only Mama and my brother could bring in money from outside so it was a hard time. Matters worsened when a neighbour with whom Papa also had some history renewed an old claim for our land. The Red Guards had once recommended expanding the local commune into our farm, but the plan had been quietly forgotten. Unfortunately our neighbour had found a good connection with a local land officer who was persuaded to award Papa's land to the commune, exactly as the guards had once threatened.

When Papa's land, our family home for as long as we knew, became 'forfeit for the greater good of the people of Dongguan', an era in my life ended.

Rather than stay in the area, searching for what Papa called false work, Papa moved us into an industrial district on the eastern edges of Guangzhou. Papa built basic relations with lower level officials and secured a small urban family unit. Into this we squeezed: four of us plus two elderly relatives on Papa's side.

It was unwelcoming accommodation. We never had money to make it as nice as our old home in Dongguan.

Officials said that I was eligible to go to a city school, but Papa wanted me and my brother to work instead. Mama looked unhappy when we came home, tired and weary from collecting urine and excrement for distribution to farmers, it was the only job we could find, but it seemed Papa had resigned himself to living off our earnings.

After complaints from Mama, Papa decided we should try reaching Hong Kong.

'At least there we'll avoid liars and cheats who hold grudges when you criticise them,' he finally said one night. It was his old tune, unchanged from Dongguan, and I think that was the first time I heard Mama tell Papa directly not to exaggerate so much.

Mama promised we could take one small canvas bag each but, in the end, I had to share with my brother.

Leaving most of my clothes and shoes and other things was upsetting. Mama, too, was in silent tears when we quietly locked the door at 3am, tip-toeing to avoid the prying eyes of the Party member who lived in the large unit with a garden. I'm sure it was a few days before people missed us; the sense of neighbourliness wasn't strong in those dangerous days.

*   *   *

SHI-BANG, male cadre, 58

Gansu Province, northwest China

'We put them through school without any official papers as I kept things quiet through good relations with the education authorities.'

AFTER MY ARREST they took me to Party headquarters for my denunciation.

It was a traditional way of punishment, they said. No matter my advanced years I must stand silently in front of the senior provincial leaders and the cameramen as they delivered the verdict.

'Expelled from the Party,' they read out, as if they were speaking to the masses in Tiananmen Square instead of a few dozen people in a small room with closed windows. 'Guilty of having too many children under state and provincial family planning targets.'

'Betraying the confidence of comrades in the Party!' one of the deputies added, shouted more-like, as if I were deaf.

After hearing all that, I confessed, just as they wanted. It was true, anyway, how could I deny it?

I *did* have three children and only one had been reported to the authorities. The two youngest ones had grown up without being recorded on official records. They lived in a village where sometimes not everyone knew whose children belonged to which family. We put them through school without any official papers as I kept things quiet through good relations with the education authorities.

But some angry local villagers had reported me because of another problem. A while back I had refused to help them get compensation when their houses had been destroyed by a collapsed mine shaft; why should I have done that, they had no money to force their claim.

But they carefully bided their time and then attacked with timely criticism that my extra children proved I was anti-People and anti-social stability.

'Living proof of Party members retaining "more children, more happiness" ambitions,' they claimed. 'The poor people stay loyal to the revolution and observe the one-child policy of the central authorities!'

The Party had no choice but to act against me; elements rearing sons for old age were natural targets in those days.

The irony was that delivering news of the final punishment was the Vice-Governor of our area.

I had known him for many years and knew for sure that he had four children, three more than officially declared, just like me. I wanted to shout out as they led me out of the chamber: 'He has four children! He has *four* children!' But of course I did not. I would need his connections with the prison people to get me out quickly.

*   *   *

MEI-MEI, female lawyer, 67

Guangdong Province, southern China

'A severed hand might be worth RMB20,000, perhaps more if the cut is unclean and looks ugly.'

PROTECTING WORKERS against sleazy authorities has been a guerrilla war for me over the years.

You know, not a specific battle with a particular court or crooked leader, but still a hard and continuous series of battles.

Mostly I fought against shared thinking amongst the authorities and Party members. Anything against one of them was taken as an unpatriotic or anti-state crime against all of them.

Lying to my face was therefore a trivial offence, for the senior officials for sure. To others it didn't even appear an offence. In their minds, rebellious lawyers were 'outside persons' and had to accept lies. I'm sure some even preferred lying. Even without much at stake they would deny things or perjure themselves, or commit some other pointless deception.

Being exposed was no embarrassment. They didn't care about consequences until they were caught and stood to be punished, which was a very rare occasion, once in a thousand times perhaps, no more than that. False tears and empty self-criticisms might happen then, but they were just tricks to lessen their prison sentence.

Strangely, prosecuting corrupt officials was always easy if it got to court.

Complicated trials finished in hours, cases with ten thousand issues that in Hong Kong or the West might last for weeks or months. Usually three judges, with one leading the prosecution would sit quietly, barely awake, nodding their heads whether or not I made a point. They knew the trial only concerned how long the defendant would spend in prison. Good defending might take a few years away, but the verdict was always known before.

The newspapers were part of the problem too.

Even the private ones only reported crimes long after they happened and then only if the courts had managed to convict somebody, anybody. They could have done a hell of a lot more to help eradicate the corruption-breeding soil in the province.

But all these collective problems were unknown to me in the early days, back in the seventies when I only wanted to use the law to protect workers. And to this day I have never handled things like intellectual-property or other things that benefit foreign firms or rich people.

Even though protecting workers was given prominence in state policies my work soon became unpopular with provincial officials.

Their first attack was to create false complaints about my qualifications. A legal department in Guangzhou ordered me to close due to illegal qualifications. At the same time their cronies tried to remove firewood from my cooking pot by spreading bad words. After a few months it felt like every dog in the Pearl River Delta was barking against me and my firm.

Thankfully an intermediate law court, one with no connections to my attackers, ruled it was legal by state rules to practice law in Guangzhou even though I had studied and qualified in Shanghai and

Hong Kong. Which, by the way, is a very positive message for lawyers anywhere in China.

After they realised they couldn't close me down that way, though, the authorities tried another attack, this time spreading rumours amongst their business cronies that I was scaring away investors. My work was actually anti-people. Of course they didn't mention that many officials or their bosses had connections with the foreign factory owners so there was a lot of self-interest and anti-people aspects to *their* approach.

In response I started to do 'class-action' work, supporting several dozen workers in a single case. My biggest case came in the late eighties and concerned fourteen female workers who had been strip-searched and generally abused at a Taiwanese-owned factory near Guangzhou. The deputy manager had also placed spy cameras in their toilet so it was a sexual case too.

The resulting media attention embarrassed city leaders greatly who wanted to keep the Taiwanese owners happy.

Despite their efforts they saw I could still defeat them and they went mad. Even the Party newspapers were forced to break their silence, aggressively criticising the 'inhuman treatment' by so-called compatriots.

Eventually the Taiwanese trade representative in Hong Kong issued a statement saying companies must observe decent working conditions in Guangdong Province. The workers received RMB5,000 in compensation each, which was a good victory in those days.

Officials then tried a third approach against me, playing 'release the enemy for recapture' type of tricks, offering hopes, false of course, that they might support some of my work.

Mid-level officials visited with offers of 'a new relationship', as they usually called it, and better communications and more private meetings to discuss workers grievances. Good connections with their bosses would make life easier for everyone. There were no guarantees, of course, but was it not my duty and responsibility to handle things this way?

Wasted time.

I could easily spot their old-fashioned tricks: all they wanted was self-censorship so they could quietly tell their cronies that they had silenced me. So our conversations always proceeded the same way: 'My position must surely be familiar to you? We are meant to be Communist, to look after the workers. That's what I grew up thinking anyway.'

'And us too, Ms Leung,' they would reply, politely and respectfully, like I was some sort of God, though of course they meant it in a quite different way. It made me laugh.

'And that is why I practice law,' I might explain if I was in the right mood. 'The Party used to say workers in Taiwan or America or Britain had no rights, only capitalist abuse by a few rich people. But in fact their workers have good protection. Are such laws not good also for our workers?'

And then they would usually claim confusion, which was un-surprising. Questioning the Party's proletarian oratory was shocking and unfathomable to people like them. Their mouth would freeze like ice and they disappeared to tell their bosses of my bad words and uncooperative attitude, like dogs running away from butchers.

For the brave little dogs, the ones that might stay a little longer, I would clarify how a defendant was innocent until proven guilty in the West, but workers in Guangdong Province, probably all China, if they ended up in court then there was the false and dangerous presumption that they must have been up to some bad deeds. I would ask how they might feel if they were in such a situation.

Of course they couldn't recognise the irony. They were high-up enough to never fear justice. In their world, and that of their cronies, the authorities were good enough already to the workers. Deng's promises of economic reform and socialism with Chinese characteristics had come true, that's what they honestly thought, and lawyers like me were just troublemakers and anti-patriotic elements.

Hopelessly blind and stupid.

It wasn't just higher-ups and their staff causing problems.

By the early nineties, more and more cases concerned workers abused by unions or worker associations that were meant to protect them.

Many senior workers saw that money could be made in the economic reforms and built advanced relations with the bosses to see if they could share in those gains. Frequently this meant financial rewards if they kept workers quiet.

The most common cases were union representatives supporting withholding overtime pay or wages for long periods. As back-payments built, bosses gained even more power over the workers.

Some of the worst offenders were workers' representatives in foreign-run factories, not only Taiwanese but South Korean and American. Even though they made items of fun for people in the West, toys and fashionable clothing and electronics, workers earned so little, less than RMB50 per day sometimes, whilst facing very dangerous conditions. Their representatives hardly cared and that made me the angriest.

I particularly remember one confrontation with a worker's leader in Shenzen.

It ended in a great shouting match at some meeting or other where I was trying to help: 'I am a dragon who looks after workers in the best way possible, by creating economic safety!' he shouted, careful not to claim that he created great economic *rewards* for the workers because he knew that was a lie.

I screamed back in frustration: 'Dragons in ancient times never breathed corrupting fire! They were wise and caring, guarding the wind and the rain and the rivers!'

It shut him up, a little, and he retreated rather than confront me further in front of the workers But he was far from defeated: 'Let's avoid sweeping outside the bit fronting our houses,' he said quietly at the end of the meeting, and as he walked away some of his crony workers who had overheard laughed. It was a psychological victory for him and his position was hardly challenged.

Some victories still happened though.

By the late nineties I had supported over ten thousand people in over one thousand cases.

I don't know the exact money won because I couldn't keep records easily. Sometimes judges ordered me to keep quiet about awards for fear of 'harming the business climate'. But compensation for common injuries like severed fingers or hands increased. A severed hand was once worth RMB20,000, perhaps more if the cut was unclean or ugly, though each court gave different money and applied different standards, especially if somebody had connections with officials.

The authorities hated when I started contingency work, something I had seen in America, where no-win, no-fee helped many poor workers to afford lawyers.

Sometimes I reduced my contingency fee to ten per cent of awards, though I didn't even take that for poorer victims. Of course this made me even more popular with the workers; and even more unpopular with the authorities.

At one stage I had over twenty people living with me. As well as feeding them I arranged for doctors to treat injuries, the kind of thing that the Party promised it would do for the people.

When a newspaper ran an article about injured workers living with me, one of whom was a triple amputee from a metal-cutting machine, an official from the lands department trumped up an eviction notice, promising 'severe legal punishment for helping troublemakers'. That had no legal basis by Guangdong's provincial residential laws, but I still had to file an appeal and that took time and money I might have spent on the workers. It was one more invisible link of loyalty between authorities; I had no history with those lands officials so why did they attack me?

After the eviction problems finished I got involved with a well-known labour activist demanding prison authorities treat his health problems caused by a previous jail term. It was so serious — he had extremely bad lungs — that I recommended a short hunger strike so we could get some press coverage in Hong Kong.

Somebody saw the articles and trumped up charges about 'subversion of state power'. Officials ruled he must return to prison 'for a certain time', though they never said how long, wrongly claiming this was consistent with state laws. What laws?

Unfortunately punishment didn't stop there. His brother was sentenced to two years, 're-education through labour', for helping advertise the counter-state activity; he was also criticised for 'speaking to foreign journalists' even though Hong Kong was part of China by then. An ex-prisoner organisation that they helped was banned. It was tough in prison; they were often held in solitary confinement and regularly beaten despite their injuries. Reading their smuggled notes made me very sad and even emotionally unbalanced . . . at times I wondered why bother, they might as well be in the *laogai*. People were suffering so much. . . .

The hunger-strike episode blew over but it created even more cases for me.

Amongst other things I supported hundreds of textile workers who had occupied a factory near Foshan. The workers insisted my team join their occupation and I could not refuse. When the fighting happened, police beat workers with steel pipes and bad sprays and other chemicals, sending several hundred to hospital, including myself. Hospital as a patient and not a visitor reminded me even more of the injustice in Guangdong Province. For weeks afterwards I wore black clothes in memory of those who died from their beatings.

I started helping younger people.

Many rural teenagers had their naïveté badly exploited in the cities. They were often forced to live in factory compounds, with all the pressures this creates, yet were banned from forming unions or committees that could try to improve conditions. If they took up a problem with their manager they were fired. Or, if the security person wasn't happy, he might beat one without a second thought for their young bodies.

One of the most absurd successes, if you can call it an achievement, was when some local officials told me it was rude for them to refuse bribes. Rude? Can you believe that? However, they established special bank accounts for anonymous deposits of bribes received. I could distribute the money to the poor workers exactly as I wanted; they kept saying 'exactly as I wanted' again and again, like repeating something three time times meant I supported their deceit. Nobody in my firm has seen any real money arrive in that account, by the way.

I'm in my sixties now and will leave this earth soon. By some laws I should be long retired.

Thankfully, others in my company are becoming strong and I'm confident they will follow my work, though I'm not sure if they'll have an easier time.

At times I wonder how long before the old imperial-style bureaucratic system dies? Traditional China seems as alive today, at least in Guangdong Province, as it was when I started my work in the seventies. I sometimes think that we are like ants on a millstone, powerless to affect anything much. And I don't know when the authorities and bureaux and agencies will stop hating and playing tricks on lawyers like me . . . and just for supporting the workers too. Where is their justice, their compassion?

*   *   *

LIU-FENG, mother, 72

Hunan Province, central China

'The worst punishment is that she can't have more children, so we've no grandchildren to look after us in old age. . . .'

WHEN OUR DAUGHTER disappeared we thought she had gone to the city for work and would soon return. Village people can be like that and she did something similar during Lunar New Year.

But after a week she had not returned and we searched for more information in Changsha. Nothing could be found.

Reporting Siu-Feng's disappearance was when we first felt something was wrong. The local police were unhelpful, believing she left deliberately or there were bad feelings between us. Senior officers told my husband new policies prevented police interfering with 'trivial family matters'. None of the state's business.

When we tried the City Affairs Office, hoping they could force police investigations, they too were quiet. An official shrugged, saying 'Young women behave strangely.'

A whole year passed, during which time we lost hope that Siu-Feng was alive, before we received an anonymous letter. It said bad elements had kidnapped Siu-Feng and other young women to sell to rich men near Hangzhou. It was devastating news, an arrow through our hearts.

During our first visit to Zhejiang Province nothing could be found. The cities felt unfamiliar and unwelcoming. Eventually, friendly sources passed on rumours about women that had appeared as wives in a nearby town.

Siu-Feng was in a terrible state. . . .

Her 'husband', Mr Wang, was quite rich but kept her in a straw hut under a bridge, about ten minutes walk from his real house.

He had beaten and raped our daughter.

Stories emerged that he had used connections with the hospital to forcibly inject her with strange liquids — we never found out what — that silenced Siu-Feng's mouth and killed her spirit.

After a year of living like that some mental illness was inevitable. She had had a troublesome birth too, without being in hospital, she must have felt great pain.

It was inconceivable that neighbours had not complained to the authorities. Was Siu-Feng's situation like the east wind passing by the horse's ear? They should have ignored Mr Wang's wealth and his good connections. They should have spoken up.

Police and other officials were bad to us. They freed Siu-Feng but refused to cut the padlock around her feet until Mr Wang gave permission. They could not find the baby boy either, though Siu-Feng didn't care, which was a heartbreaking sign of her abuse and terrible suffering.

Mr Wang claimed Siu-Feng stayed under the bridge voluntarily. He had even given her good money but she had insisted . . . terrible lies, which the locks on her feet challenged. But Mr Wang was unashamed: 'After *your* lies,' he finished, 'I want nothing to do with her. Take her away! Make these people leave!'

The authorities supported him as if he was their father and asked us to go to avoid future problems.

As we travelled back to Hunan Province without the baby, who still couldn't be found, least of all by the police, I knew in my heart Siu-Feng would never be right again. We were determined to find the guilty parties in our area.

The police remained unhelpful, even when other stories emerged from other families, but months later shifted their position back-to-front.

It was during a large anti-crime campaign, as I remember, something initiated by state authorities as part of the Strike Hard campaign. Suddenly officials were concerned about unhappy marriages and family violence. Many sweet words surfaced: 'In the process of economic growth,' an official assured us. 'The social status of some women has lowered, especially in poorer provinces like Hunan.'

From now on the Party and their supporters would make a greater interference in marriage and other family matters. The Party wanted to end the idea that Siu-Feng's experience was beyond the reach of law. 'Crimes like this must be punished!'

Somebody higher-up in the Party eventually proved guilty elements had identified attractive women and told the villains where to catch them.

The women had been locked in cages on curtained buses, going for days on tiny amounts of water and food, like trapped bears. If they screamed out they used cattle prods to shock them to silence. No wonder Siu-Feng never talked about it.

About a month later the newspapers said a deputy-governor connected with several crimes like this had been purged from the Party.

He and his cronies had taken nearly RMB3 million in bribes over the years, though details of the charge weren't publicised widely so we never knew which villages or towns were affected.

For abusing his Party privileges and connections with senior figures in Beijing the deputy-governor was sentenced to death; they said it was the most important execution in Hunan since the Cultural Revolution. Official newspapers rallied against the *zhufan,* major criminals, which made us feel confident that the authorities did look after poor people in the end. We would receive some money from those millions for our suffering.

But no money appeared.

When another vice-chairman who had managed to escape the first round of arrests was given a life sentence we felt the money would appear; he was the one who paid police to ignore complaints and go slow on investigations. Surely we would get some financial compensation this time.

But this second punishment led to nothing and we were not compensated.

And all we have now is the cold satisfaction of knowing about the punishment of officials, which won't bring back our daughter's health.

Siu-Feng's like a ghost, really. She is frightened to leave the house and stares into the sky often . . . our punishment is that she can't have more children, there were some injuries from the first birth, so we have no grandchildren to look after us in old age.

Meanwhile, the money those senior people made has disappeared like the life from a pig with no throat, only a wound. So what can we think? Only that people at the highest levels can plunge the lowest depths.

*　　　*　　　*

afterword

THIRTY VOICES can never do justice to the kaleidoscope of China's conflicts. China is too big and too varied. But *Broken Dragons* illuminates, I hope, some common themes that underlie life in China today.

The first, and most vital, is that people in China, like everybody else, approach problems from individual and very personal perspectives. Some rich Chinese approach trouble very aggressively, either proactively or reactively, but I also saw others who were conciliatory and kind. Some poor struck me as willing participants in the dishonesty of wealthier offenders whilst some were anything but. Some elderly were clearly involved with suspicious money and illicit careerism, but others sinned only by omission and not commission.

Second, almost all tend to search for the good in a situation, or at least for workable solutions.

These stories illustrate a pragmatic approach to conflict. Where the Red Guards forcibly resettled millions, other revolutionaries have been far more tolerant and quiet. I can understand why Tiananmen Square in 1989 had its roots in the 1986 protest for democracy that was handled more or less peacefully. Cross-straits peace has held for two generations. Despite the political invective, the reality of

Chinese-Taiwan relations is an accommodating status quo; both sides know that what is said and what is meant are different things.

Many err towards a less assorted view of China's conflicts and corruption, blinding themselves to the possibilities that can be found in situations that at first seem hopeless and desperate. Many stories in *Broken Dragons* offer reasons for optimism and show there is a deeply felt awareness about what constitutes 'justice', in the sense of 'what is the decent thing'.

Where one person looks to 'fight poison with poison' another slews towards 'making a direct apology'; where one seeks to 'hold fast in controlling destinies over foreigners' others run away.

Problems arose from the spectrum of human emotions: jealousy, envy of money, families growing apart, prejudice towards national enemies, disparate educational levels, revenge.

The people I talked with for Broken Dragons renewed my admiration for the communists' attempts to reduce the influence of Confucianism, especially the 'three bonds': subject-to-ruler; son-to-father; wife-to-husband. In the communist view this imposed a great claustrophobia on much of China. Unfortunately the elimination of Confucianism has been superficial, at best, and it is sad to say that the rules of protocol remain adamantine in a lot of China. It is also clear that, ironically and I am sure unintentionally, problems have been worsened by the cadre system's countless nuances of rank, from state-governor to white-collar workers to workers' representatives, many defined by when somebody first joined the Communist Party. It was easy to find memories of the Cultural Revolution when the country was divided into as many as 30,000 communes dominated by often brutal 'local emperors'.

Many of the messy conflicts and cases of corruption depicted in these pages have been resolved with rather canny solutions, and left me optimistic that this sensible management of conflict can benefit the wider Chinese landscape.

Above all, after writing *Broken Dragons,* I understand more why China's ruling elite survived Tiananmen Square, the 1997 Asian crisis and SARS without seeming to make much concession if any to the democratic cause. But if there is a Damoclean sword hanging over the long-term future of China, I would say that it is the absence of democracy.

CPSIA information can be obtained at www.ICGtesting.com
Printed in the USA
LVOW091511150212

268853LV00005B/14/A

9 789628 674039